"What do you think you're doing, McGill?"

J.D. tried to look over her shoulder, but Luke gently grabbed her head and turned it back.

"I'm going to massage your neck and shoulders and hopefully ease your headache. That is—" he leaned forward, his mouth close to her ear "—unless you've found your aspirin."

He felt the little shiver that ran down her spine. It paralleled his own. Damn, this was a complication he didn't want in his life. His ex-wife had taught him that he was no good with relationships. And he definitely didn't want a relationship with J. D. Anderson, good or bad.

Now sex—that was a different matter.

You're really losing it now, McGill, if you think she would let you near her.

And yet, it was hard to think of anything else.

Dear Reader,

It's another great month for Silhouette Intimate Moments! If you don't believe me, just take a look at our American Hero title, *Dragonslayer,* by Emilie Richards. This compelling and emotionally riveting tale could have been torn from today's headlines, with a minister hero whose church is in one of the inner city's worst neighborhoods and whose chosen flock includes the down and out of the world. In this place, where gang violence touches everyone's lives—and will continue to touch them throughout the book in ways you won't be able to predict—our hero meets a woman whose paradoxical innocence will force him to confront his own demons, his own inner emptiness, and once more embrace life—and love. *Dragonslayer* is a *tour de force,* not to be missed by any reader.

The rest of the month is terrific, too. Marilyn Pappano, Doreen Roberts, Marion Smith Collins, Beverly Barton and new author Leann Harris offer stories that range from "down-home" emotional to suspenseful and dramatic. You'll want to read them all.

And in months to come look for more irresistible reading from such favorite authors as Justine Davis, Linda Turner, Paula Detmer Riggs, *New York Times* bestsellers Heather Graham Pozzessere and Nora Roberts, and more—all coming your way from Silhouette Intimate Moments, where romantic excitement is always the rule.

Yours,

Leslie J. Wainger
Senior Editor and Editorial Coordinator

BRIDE
ON THE RUN

Leann
Harris

Silhouette®

INTIMATE ▼ **MOMENTS®**

Published by Silhouette Books New York

America's Publisher of Contemporary Romance

SILHOUETTE BOOKS
300 East 42nd St., New York, N.Y. 10017

BRIDE ON THE RUN

Copyright © 1993 by Leann Harris

All rights reserved. Except for use in any review, the reproduction
or utilization of this work in whole or in part in any form by any
electronic, mechanical or other means, now known or hereafter
invented, including xerography, photocopying and recording, or in
any information storage or retrieval system, is forbidden without
the permission of the publisher, Silhouette Books, 300 E. 42nd St.,
New York, N.Y. 10017

ISBN: 0-373-07516-2

First Silhouette Books printing August 1993

All the characters in this book have no existence outside the
imagination of the author and have no relation whatsoever to
anyone bearing the same name or names. They are not even
distantly inspired by any individual known or unknown to the
author, and all incidents are pure invention.

®: Trademark used under license and registered in the United States
Patent and Trademark Office and in other countries.

Printed in the U.S.A.

LEANN HARRIS

When Leann Harris first met her husband in college, she never dreamed she would marry him. After all, he was getting a Ph.D. in the one science she'd managed to avoid—physics! So much for first impressions. They have now been happily married for over twenty years. After graduating from the University of Texas at Austin, Leann taught math and science to deaf high school students until the birth of her first child. It wasn't until her youngest child started school that Leann decided to fulfill a lifelong dream and began writing. She presently lives in Plano, Texas, with her husband, two children and her Boston terrier, Grizzly.

My thanks to the following people who were instrumental in helping me with this book:

Sgt. Jim Chandler, Lt. David Davis, Jr., and Detective Cheryl Palmer of the Dallas police department for their generous sharing of time and information.

Judy Christenberry, Karen Morrell, Karen Leabo, Ann Franklin and Dana Lindsey for their insights and feedback.

My husband, Herman, and my children, Jennifer and Daniel, who learned to leave mother alone when she's at the computer.

My parents, especially my mom, whose indomitable spirit and loving heart were the inspiration for J. D. Anderson.

Chapter 1

Lucas McGill stared out his office window at the shriveled tree in the parking lot below. He resisted the urge to ram his fist through the window and vent his frustration. Stuffing his hands into his back pockets, he glanced over his shoulder at the papers lying on his desk. The ballistics report on the slug they'd gotten out of Marion Glass was inconclusive. In other words, they couldn't prove the bullet that had killed the wealthy Dallas socialite came from her husband's gun. But it was as obvious as Rayford Glass's oily smile that he'd killed his wife.

Lucas turned and walked back to his desk. Without that piece of evidence, their case against the charming, charismatic Rayford was completely circumstantial. All the man had to do was hire a high-priced lawyer to cast a few doubts in the jury's mind, and the sleazebag would go free. It was enough to make a good cop want to throw in his badge.

Needing to get away from his desk, Luke grabbed his coffee mug and left the office. Three steps into the squad room, he heard his nemesis—then saw her.

"What makes you think something has happened to your friend?" David Sanders, the officer in charge of missing persons, asked her.

"Because when she talked to me about three hours ago she sounded agitated."

David shrugged. "So, lots of people get upset on the phone and then decide not to go through with their plans."

The petite blonde carefully placed her hands on the desk and leaned forward, giving Luke a clear view of her enticing backside. Much to his surprise and disgust, a jolt of electricity hit him square in the gut, making his palms itch and his pulse accelerate.

He cursed under his breath. If there was one thing that really irritated him, it was being attracted to a woman he actively disliked.

Folding his arms across his chest, he leaned against the wall in anticipation of what the lady's response would be. If his past experience with the woman was any indication, his friend was about to discover why the boys down in investigation called her "The Terminator."

"Lieutenant, when Gwen called me she said she had information that would shake this state's government to its core. She was scared and in need of a lawyer. I don't think she suddenly decided things were all hearts and flowers. I think someone found out what she was up to and stopped her. Now, unless you want it revealed that the woman who uncovered the biggest scandal in state history was reported missing and the Dallas Police Department sat on their hands and did nothing, I suggest you issue a missing persons report on her.''

Luke grinned. Yup, the lady lawyer was up to form. Ready to tear a man's leg off and beat him to death with it. He ought to know. He had tangled with her in court on three occasions and had been the winner only once.

Her knockout good looks, combined with her generous curves and sexy smile, made a man think she was soft, vulnerable, in need of protection. Hah! What a crock that was. She was about as defenseless as a rattlesnake. He clearly remembered the first time he had faced her in court. Since she was the defense lawyer, he'd been wary of her, but she'd smiled and said hello in a voice so low and intimate that he lowered his guard for an instant. Then she sucker-punched him. Her questioning was fierce, hard and smart, and he'd come out looking like an officer who had a score to settle with the defendant. Never mind that it was true. The important thing was the punk was guilty of robbing the liquor store and beating up the manager.

''Give me the missing woman's name and address.'' David's request cut through Luke's wandering thoughts.

''Gwen Kennedy.''

''Address.''

When she didn't answer, Luke carefully studied her face. If he didn't know better, he would've sworn that she was blushing. Surely not. Arnold Schwarzenegger never blushed.

''What's her address?'' David asked again.

Clearing her throat, she said, ''I'm not sure.''

''What do you mean you're not sure?''

She drew herself up to her towering five-foot-one-inch height. "I mean I have no earthly idea where Gwen lives. When I was home last July fourth, I saw her at a party, but we only exchanged hellos. Other than that, I haven't heard from her since high school, which was close to eighteen years ago."

David leaned back in his chair, eyes wide with incredulity. "Do you have any idea what she did for a living?"

"No."

"Do you know if she was married?"

"No."

"Does she have any family in the area that could help?"

"No. We grew up in Midland. Her father died a few years ago. Her brother left home the year before she graduated, and I don't think she ever heard from him again."

David shook his head. "Do you at least have a picture of her? Can you give us a description?"

Luke noted with each question how the expression on her beautiful face grew harder and harder. Obviously she knew she had little to go on, but that very fact only emphasized how much she felt the missing woman was in danger. J.D. Anderson was a pain in the butt, but she knew her law and didn't raise any false alarms.

Unable to stop himself, Luke crossed the room to David's desk. "Hello, Ms. Anderson."

"Detective McGill." Although she said his name with cool formality, the timbre of her voice made him think of dark nights, satin sheets and hot bodies. He gritted his teeth. It was one of the things that irritated him the most about J.D. Anderson. Personally, he didn't like her. Too bad his body did.

"I couldn't help but overhear your conversation with Lieutenant Sanders. Where were you supposed to meet Ms. Kennedy?"

"In the lobby of the World Trade Center about one o'clock."

"How long did you wait?"

"An hour. I have a court case in less than thirty minutes, so I couldn't wait any longer."

He noted the trace of annoyance in her voice. "Were you late for the meeting? Maybe she left before you got there."

"I was late by five minutes."

The fire in her eyes told him she didn't appreciate him implying it was her fault she and Gwen failed to connect.

"Why don't you give David a description of your friend—"

"Client."

Standing corrected, Luke nodded. "—your client, and we'll put out a missing person's bulletin on her."

"Thank you, Detective."

Her caustic tone sliced him to the quick. "You're welcome, Counselor Anderson."

Luke strode to the coffee machine while J.D. gave the description. When David finished taking the report, he joined Luke.

"Whoa, for such a little thing, she packs a mean punch," he muttered, grabbing his coffee mug.

Luke grinned.

David leaned close. "I heard she eats cops for lunch."

Luke's eyes were drawn to the woman waiting for the elevator. "You don't know the half of it." The conservative navy business suit she wore couldn't disguise her womanly curves. The elevator opened and, with a gentle sway of her hips, she walked inside and turned. Her eyes met his. A spark arced between them and he felt his blood surge. What was the matter with him? he wondered sourly, grinding his teeth. He should be investigating the Glass murder instead of standing here gaping at a woman like a sixteen-year-old.

The headlights of her battered compact fell on the two strips of concrete that served as her driveway. She parked the car before the detached garage in her backyard. Too tired to bother putting her car in the garage, she gathered her purse and briefcase and started toward the house. One of these days she would get around to buying an automatic garage-door opener.

What a wretched day it had been. Immigration Services had ruled against the Ramos family and the parents were to be deported, leaving their three children, ages three, eighteen months, and four months, with relatives here in the States. Then Gwen had called, desperate and in need of help. A gut feeling told J.D. that something very wrong had happened to her high school friend.

And then there had been her accidental meeting with Supercop himself, Lucas McGill. His reputation was legendary. Tough. Hard. Nerves of steel. Unshakable when questioned. A royal pain. Just the mention of his name elicited a moan from most attorneys. Nobody wanted to face him in court. The first time she'd questioned him, he'd proved the other lawyers right. He'd been a hard case.

Lucas McGill was the embodiment of all the male characteristics she disliked. A Neanderthal with a badge. Unfortunately, his whiskey colored eyes sparked something strange inside her.

"J.D. Whoa, J.D."

Hearing the screen on the neighbor's door slam, she turned to find her friend Sarah Miller running down the steps.

"I'm so glad you're home," Sarah panted as she came to a stop beside J.D.

"Is something wrong?" The worries of the day disappeared in the face of her friend's distress.

"Yes. A notice came in the mail today that the IRS is going to audit us."

"That shouldn't be a problem. Is it?"

Sarah shrugged and looked down at her sandals. "Everything Larry claimed is true. It's just that we didn't keep all the necessary paperwork the government requires."

Knowing her neighbor's husband, she didn't doubt their predicament. "Sarah, I don't know a thing about tax law."

Sarah's head snapped up. "No, but you might know a good tax lawyer."

"You're right. I know the best tax lawyer in town. I don't remember his number. Come on inside and I'll get it for you."

"Let me go turn off my spaghetti sauce. Then I'll be right over."

J.D. unlocked the back door and walked through the kitchen, down the long hall to what once was the living room, now her office. She flicked on the lights, then froze at the sight that greeted her. Her filing cabinets had been ransacked, their contents flung about the room. In stunned disbelief, she walked to her desk. The drawers hung out drunkenly, spilling papers, rubber bands and paper clips onto the floor. Even her mail, which her secretary always placed neatly on the desk, had been ripped open, then tossed aside. Yet, oddly enough, her diamond watch sat in the middle of the chaos.

Hearing a noise from the corner of the room, she spun around. She didn't get a clear picture of the man before his fist slammed into her jaw. As the darkness swallowed her, her last thought connected this new disaster with Gwen Kennedy.

As he left the parking garage, Luke turned on his police radio. He was off duty, but it didn't hurt to know what the guys on the evening shift were handling. Routine things, shootings, domestic disturbances, burglaries. He'd stopped for a light when the call came in for a patrol car and ambulance to go to a familiar Swiss Avenue address.

J.D. Anderson's house.

After the last time he'd tangled with her in court, he called up her address on the police computer and went by just to see, he assured himself, what kind of a house the cold, heartless female lived in. He'd been surprised. The modest two-story frame structure, recently remodeled, didn't fit his image of the daughter of a wealthy West Texas oilman. The restored mansions farther down the street were more in line with his image of her.

This time he didn't drive by, but parked on the opposite side of the street. After showing his badge to the uniformed officer at the front door, he entered the living room. He carefully noted the condition of the room. J.D. sat on the sofa, a paramedic kneeling before her, taking her blood pressure. Another woman hovered at the end of the sofa. He couldn't remember ever seeing J.D. in such a disheveled condition. Several long blond strands of hair had escaped the bun at the back of her head. The shirttail of her silky-looking blouse hung over the waistband of her expensive suit. She was missing one shoe.

J.D. looked up and her eyes collided with his.

A second uniformed cop strode into the room. "Luke, what are you doing here?" He turned to J.D. "You did tell me everything, didn't you? No one was murdered here?"

From the fire blazing in her blue eyes, Luke guessed that if the perpetrator was within J.D.'s reach, he really would have a murder on his hands. He'd bet his last five bucks that Counselor Anderson wouldn't be defending this particular offender.

"No, Mike, this isn't an official visit. I saw the squad car, knew the lady and decided to see if I could help."

"Well, I'll be d—" Mike bit down on the word after glancing at his friend.

Luke stepped closer to the officer. "Don't read anything into this."

"Of course I won't." Mike tried to look innocent.

The paramedic snapped his bag closed. "That's all I can do for you, miss. I wish you'd let us take you to the hospital to check for a concussion."

"The man just hit me in the jaw and knocked me out."

"There could be complications."

"I seriously doubt there will be any, except maybe a bruise. I'm too hardheaded. Isn't that right, Detective McGill?"

Luke's eyes narrowed on the darkening area of J.D.'s chin. The lady had taken a good wallop and suddenly he wanted to get his hands on the guy who'd hurt her. "Well, if determination has anything to do with it, Ms. Anderson will be fine."

As the paramedic gathered up the rest of his gear, Luke pulled Mike aside. "What happened?"

"Ms. Anderson came in and caught an intruder going through her files."

"Did she get a good look at him?"

"Nope. The only thing she saw clearly was a gloved fist before it punched her out."

"Any signs of forced entry?"

"Yeah. The side window."

"Anything missing?"

"Hard to tell in here. Nothing was touched upstairs."

Out of the corner of his eye, Luke saw J.D. stand, then stagger. Instantly, he shot across the space that separated them and grabbed her arm before she could fall. Her momentum carried her into him. He felt every inch of her incredibly soft body, from her shoulders to her hips. For an instant the rest of the room faded, and his gaze locked with a pair of deep blue eyes.

She must have felt the same sizzle that burned up his spine. Judging from her expression and sudden jerking away, she didn't like the sensation any more than he did.

An awkward silence filled the room. Their little exchange had been witnessed by the two uniformed officers, the paramedic and the other woman.

Well, if you're going to make a total fool of yourself, McGill, might as well have an audience.

It was obvious that if he wanted to get out of this situation skin-intact and not be fodder for the police grapevine, he was going to have to redirect everyone's attention. He looked at J.D. "Is this the first time you've been robbed?"

"Oh, no," the other woman answered, stepping to J.D.'s side. "This is the fourth time. And Larry and I—we live next door—we've been burglarized three times. Why, you'd think in this neighborhood of old, respected homes that the police could do a better job of protecting the citizens."

"Mike, why don't you take this lady—" Luke motioned toward the woman "—into the kitchen and take her statement."

"Sure, Luke."

J.D. slumped down onto the couch. Resting her head on the cushions, she closed her eyes and sighed. Luke walked around the fallen desk chair, resisting the urge to set it upright since the Physical Evidence Squad had not yet arrived, and sat next to J.D.

She rolled her head to the side and opened her eyes. "What are you doing here? As the patrolman said, nobody was murdered."

"I heard the call on my radio, was a block away and decided to come by and see if I could help."

"Now, why do I find that hard to believe?"

"Maybe because you're suspicious of every move the police make."

Never lifting her head from the cushion, she pinned him with a penetrating stare. "Do you know what I think? I think you knew whose house this was and came by to see if I got what you think I deserve."

She was partially right. He had known whose house it was, but he couldn't identify the reason he'd stopped. "As usual, Counselor, your conclusion is incorrect. We're shorthanded. Any help from a fellow officer is greatly appreciated."

She sighed and rubbed her temples. Luke's eyes were drawn to the massive bruise on her jaw. As ridiculous as it was, he wanted to soothe his fingers over the injury, wrap his arms around her and pull her close.

What kind of coward would hurt a woman, even a tough-as-nails female like J.D. Anderson? If the man was in the room right now, he'd teach the scum a thing or two about respect.

"This is not an aimless robbery like the other ones," J.D. said, interrupting his thoughts.

"Why do you say that?"

"Because the officer said nothing else was disturbed."

"Maybe you came in before the guy could work his way upstairs."

"Do you really believe that, Detective?"

He shrugged.

"How many junkies do you know who would pass up an expensive diamond watch to go through the mail and legal files?"

"What diamond watch?"

"The one on the desk. It needed a new battery, so I gave it to my secretary this morning. Apparently she got it fixed and left it where she was sure I'd find it."

Luke stood and walked to the desk. The watch was right where she said it was. He picked up the expensive piece. Any thief who'd overlooked this was searching for something besides a prize to pawn.

So where did that leave them?

He faced her. "Do you have any idea what the thief was looking for?"

"No, but I know without a shadow of a doubt that it was somehow connected with Gwen Kennedy."

He had the sinking feeling in his gut she was right.

Chapter 2

Luke had no trouble finding the crime scene on the bank of the Trinity River. Four patrol cars, the coroner's van and the evidence team car marked the spot on the grassy slope. As a matter of fact, anyone in the skyscrapers downtown couldn't have missed this circus. Too bad the murder didn't have as many witnesses as the discovery of the body did. It would've made his job easier.

Luke turned off the paved street and drove through the choppy terrain, gritting his teeth against the bone-jarring ride. There went the new alignment of his car. The moment he opened his door, the senior officer at the scene and his friend, Frank Seaman, approached.

"So you got stuck with this," Frank teased.

"Yeah, all the other detectives were out or sick, so they gave this one to me. Whatcha got, Frank?"

"The boys over there—" he nodded toward two

teens milling around a patrol car ''—were gathering aluminum cans and found the woman's body.''

Luke motioned for Frank to lead the way. ''Have you found any identification? A purse, a wallet?''

''No such luck.''

Luke carefully studied the scene while the evidence team finished taking pictures. Female, Caucasian, five-six, maybe five-seven, slender, reddish-brown hair. She lay sprawled on her stomach, an ugly bullet hole at the base of her head. The hit looked professional.

''Any evidence of sexual assault?'' If it was a professional hit, there wouldn't be any sexual overtones.

''It's hard to tell at this stage.''

Luke walked around the body, studying it from different angles. Suddenly he remembered J.D.'s description of her missing friend, which matched this body. Squatting beside the woman's face, he pulled his pen from his shirt pocket and used the tip to move her chin to the side. High on her right cheek was a mole, exactly as J.D. had described her friend Gwen Kennedy.

They would need J.D. to positively identify the body, but he was ninety-eight percent certain he'd found the counselor's missing client.

Ah, hell.

He stood, exasperated by the thought of having to deal with J.D. Anderson again. Staring down at the ground, he noticed an unusual print in the moist earth. From the shape, the pointed toe and deep heel, there was no mistaking the boot print. But it was the heel that made this print unique.

Luke looked down at Frank's feet. ''You're not wearing boots.''

"So?"

Luke motioned to him. "Come here and look at this."

Frank leaned down and examined the muddy imprint. "It's a Western boot, all right. But look at that heel. It's got the state of Texas carved in it. Have you ever seen one like that?"

Luke shook his head. "Any of your boys wearing boots?"

"I don't know. Hey, guys, anyone got on Western boots?" Frank yelled, momentarily stopping all activity. When they received a negative response, Frank grinned. "I think we've got a clue to who the killer is."

"Some lead, Frank. The guy wears boots. Half the men in Texas wear boots."

"But not boots like these. They're probably a custom job. That should narrow things down."

"Sure. Now instead of having close to a million suspects, I probably only have a hundred thousand."

Luke stepped out of the elevator the same moment J.D. walked out the courtroom doors. The familiar and definitely unwelcome charge of sexual awareness twisted his insides. Of all the females in the state, of all the lawyers out of that population, why her? It made him spitting mad.

Engaged in a lively conversation with the assistant district attorney, she failed to notice him. He took the opportunity to study her. She looked tired but not defeated. The bruise on her chin, which stood out despite her attempts to cover it with makeup, gave her a fragile quality.

Odd, he had the ridiculous impulse to reach out and comfort her, tell her that he'd catch the creep who did this to her. He shook his head in disgust. This job was getting to him. One did not comfort the Terminator, no matter if she did have a body to die for.

He stepped forward. "Afternoon, Counselor, Stewart."

The two stopped in surprise.

"Hi, Luke." Stewart Grant held out his hand. Luke shook it. "What are you doing here?"

"I was looking for Ms. Anderson, here."

Stewart's brow shot up. "Oh?"

"She reported a client missing. I think we've found the woman."

J.D.'s body seemed to sag. Her deep sigh touched him. He gritted his teeth against the feeling.

"I suppose since you're the one telling me, Detective McGill, it means Gwen's dead."

He couldn't quite identify the emotion in her voice. Pain, disappointment, discouragement.

"The body of a young woman matching the description of your client was found this morning. We need you to identify it before we can say positively that it's Gwen Kennedy."

"All right. When do you need me?"

"As soon as possible."

J.D. lightly ran her fingers over her forehead. "I'm finished here for the day. I can do it now, then go home."

"Great. I'll follow you over there."

J.D. flushed.

"Is something the matter, Counselor?"

She glanced at Stewart, then at him. "How do you feel about following a DART bus?"

"What are you talking about?"

"I rode the bus here this morning, McGill. I strongly believe in public transit. I use the bus whenever I can."

It figured. The lady defended the indigent, marched for causes, rode the bus and was a general pain in the butt. And, of course, he could just imagine the reaction of all his buddies in the department if they discovered he'd been trailing a DART bus because he couldn't convince one stubborn female to accept a ride from him.

Stewart broke out in laughter. "I can just see you, Luke, following a bus."

Although it was only a seven-minute drive from the courthouse to Parkland Hospital where the county morgue was located, it would take the better part of an hour to get there by bus with all the stops and starts it made.

"Look, Anderson—" since she'd called him by his last name, he might as well return the favor "—why don't I just give you a lift over there? That way, we'll finish that much more quickly. Okay?"

From the expression on her beautiful face, it was apparent she didn't like the idea of riding with him anywhere, but he had confidence that her practical side would win out over her distaste. It had to be a common experience for her, as many rotten defendants as she represented. He frowned at the comparison.

"All right, McGill. Lead the way."

Luke looked at Stewart. "Let me know when you need me in court on the Jameson case."

"Will do. J.D., I'll get back in touch with you later." Grinning, Stewart turned and strode down the hall. His cheerful whistle annoyed Luke. Stewart might have found the situation funny. *He* didn't.

The trip to the hospital was the longest Luke had ever made. Nothing, not a word, a syllable, a sigh passed between him and J.D. He could coin a new phrase—graveyard silence.

The Southwest Institute for Forensic Sciences, or SWIF as it was affectionately known among the police officials, was located outside the emergency door of Parkland, the main county hospital.

He parked the car, then came around and opened the passenger door. J.D. looked up in surprise. His actions surprised him, too, considering this was J.D. "hate all policemen" Anderson. He tried to shrug it off. "My mother raised me to be a gentleman," he offered by way of an explanation.

"Too bad you aren't one on the witness stand," she grumbled. She grabbed her purse and stood.

"When you're challenging my credibility as a professional, Ms. Anderson, I fight hard, bare knuckles, and I don't pull my punches."

"I know, McGill. I just assumed you were that nasty all the time."

Sometimes he just wanted to get his hands around her neck and...and what? he thought, watching the gentle sway of her hips as she walked to the door. The woman had the mouth of a shrew and the body of an angel. A bad combination.

The moment he stepped inside, one of the coroner's assistants he knew called out his name.

"Luke, what are you doing here?"

"Marv, Ms. Anderson and I came to view the body of an unidentified female they brought in this morning."

"Yeah, I remember that one. Let me see where they put her. She probably isn't in one of the drawers yet. We had a surplus of bodies over the weekend and are pretty backed up. Your body's probably still in one of the freezers."

When Luke turned around, he found J.D. sitting on a bench, her head resting against the wall, her eyes closed.

"You okay, Anderson?"

Slowly she opened her eyes. "Yes."

She was pale. Her skin appeared colorless, the life drained out of it. "You sure?"

"McGill, I have a raging headache, the smell of this place makes me want to vomit, but I'll make it."

Marvin reappeared and motioned to them. "C'mon, folks. I've got the body you want to see in the viewing room."

He watched in amazement as J.D. squared her shoulders, stood and with a regal bearing followed Marvin. She remained calm, almost detached, as she viewed the body.

"Is that Gwen Kennedy?"

J.D. met his gaze and he saw the sheen of moisture in her eyes. "Yes."

She said nothing more but simply turned and walked back to the main entrance. By the time he finished his business with Marvin, he found J.D. again seated on the bench. Her eyes were closed, her fingers slowly massaging her temples.

"I'm sorry about your friend."

She shook her head. "I knew when she didn't show for our meeting that something bad had happened. I just hoped . . ."

Suddenly, her fingers flew to the back of her head. With a practiced ease, she plucked all the pins from her bun, then shook her hair free. She ran one hand through the gold strands as she tossed the pins into her purse.

A giant, iron fist hit Luke in the stomach, taking his breath away as he watched the spill of honey blond hair fall over her shoulders to touch the wood of the bench and pool around her hips. He'd no idea that Miss "Steel Will" Anderson possessed such long, gorgeous, sexy hair.

One of the other male assistants wandered through the hall and stopped dead in his tracks when he saw J.D. Luke glared at him, and the man took the hint and moved away.

"I need something for this wretched headache."

Her voice brought his attention back to her. She threw open the black bag she called a purse and started pulling things out. His eyes grew wide as he watched her remove two chocolate bars, a peanut butter cup, several fudge drops, and a bag of candy coated chocolates. The lady had a passion for chocolate. He wondered what her other passions were.

"Where are those stupid aspirins?"

The desperation in her voice caught his attention. When she looked up at him, he saw raging pain reflected clearly in her eyes. He'd seen that look often when he was growing up. His mother had been plagued with headaches, and sometimes, before the pain became intense, if he massaged her neck and shoulders, they could avert the headache.

The thought of putting his hands on J.D.'s neck, running his fingers through her hair, had a definite effect on his body. Ignoring his own response, he said,

"Move over." He sat next to her, resting his hands on her shoulder. She jumped.

"What do you think you're doing?" She tried to look over her shoulder, but he gently grabbed her head and turned it back.

"I'm going to massage your neck and shoulders and hopefully ease your headache, that is—" he leaned forward, his mouth close to her ear "—unless you've found your aspirin."

He felt the little shiver that ran down her spine. It paralleled his own. Damn, this was a complication he didn't want in his life. His ex-wife taught him that he was no good with relationships. And he definitely didn't want a relationship with the counselor, good or bad.

Now, sex—that was a different matter.

You're really losing it now, McGill, if you think that J.D. Anderson would let you near her.

And yet, it was hard to think of anything else as he slowly ran his hands up her neck, his fingers spearing into her thick hair.

A tiny moan slipped from her lips, making the muscles of his stomach tighten.

"Where did you learn to give such wonderful massages?"

"I used to give my mother massages for her headaches. My ex-wife said it was the only thing I knew how to do right."

She went still under his hands. "You were married?"

The wonderment in her voice annoyed him. He pulled his hands away from her neck and stood.

"Yeah, Anderson, there was one woman fool enough to marry me. Obviously she wised up because she divorced me." He turned away.

"McGill."

He stopped.

"I didn't mean it the way it sounded. It's just that I've never thought of you as married."

He glanced over his shoulder. Her sincere expression convinced him that she hadn't meant anything nasty. "Apparently neither did my ex-wife. Gather up your things, Counselor, and I'll drive you home."

He didn't wait to see if she did. He pushed open the door and walked to his car.

Amazingly, her headache eased. She had to agree with McGill's ex-wife. He gave a first-rate massage. Maybe he had missed his calling by becoming a policeman. No, in spite of the aggravation he caused her, McGill was a good cop. In fact, she was glad he was the investigating officer on Gwen's case.

She glanced over at him behind the wheel of the unmarked police car. In anybody's book, McGill was a drop-dead handsome man. Women probably weren't falling all over themselves to get to him because of the hard set to his jaw and the chilling way he greeted most people.

It was difficult to imagine him married. She regretted her reaction to his little announcement. She hadn't meant to be rude. Whenever she thought about him— which she rarely did, she hurriedly assured herself— she always envisioned him as single. By his own admission, he wasn't good husband material.

Why on earth was she thinking about him as husband material? That headache really must have scrambled her brain.

She leaned her head on the seat back. A shiver caught her by surprise as she remembered the feel of his callused, hard fingers on her neck. She had wanted to melt into his strength, lose herself in the pleasure.

Her head snapped up.

"You okay, Anderson?" He glanced at her.

"Yes."

"You look like you remembered something important."

Or wanted to avoid a dangerous thought. "No, nothing like that."

"When we get to your house, I'd like to question you about Gwen, see what we can come up with."

"I take it she had no identification with her when she was found."

"No such luck."

He turned into her driveway and parked behind her battered fifteen-year-old clunker. Arching his brow, he looked at her. "Is that hunk of cr—junk yours?"

"You bet."

"Would you mind telling me why the daughter of one of the wealthiest oilmen in the state drives that?"

She shrugged. "My expensive convertible was stolen the second day I lived here. Nobody touches this car, no matter what part of Dallas I park in."

He laughed. The surprising sound was rich and full, causing the oddest flutter in J.D.'s stomach.

"You amaze me, Counselor," he said. He slammed the car door shut and followed her inside. "Nobody in the department will believe that the Terminator has a sense of humor."

J.D. whirled in time to see him freeze when he realized what he'd said. If she didn't know better, she'd swear that he was blushing. Naw, couldn't be.

"Don't worry about it, McGill. I know about the little nickname. Someday remind me to tell you what the defense attorneys call you."

"They have a name for me?" he asked, following her down the hall to her office.

She paused, taking off both her high heels. "Yeah, and it's a gem." Before he could ask any other questions, she greeted her secretary. "Hi, Emma. Anything happen while I was gone?"

Emma stared over her shoulder. "Who's the hunk?"

J.D. glanced back, thinking perhaps someone else had entered the room. "Who?"

"Him," Emma stated, pointing at McGill.

J.D. leaned close to Emma's ear. "He's a cop."

"What did you do now, J.D.?"

With a dramatic sigh, J.D. shook her head. "I really ought to fire you, Emma."

Emma gave a short laugh. "Sure, and it's going to snow here in July." She first studied J.D. from the top of her head to her stocking-clad feet, then the detective. "What exactly have you been doing this afternoon?"

"Detective McGill took me to the morgue to identify Gwen Kennedy's body."

Emma came out of her chair. "I'm sorry, J.D. I had no idea. I was just thrilled to see you looking mussed in the company of a gorgeous man."

J.D. tried to stop her cheeks from flaming. She might as well have tried to stop the sun from coming up. Why didn't Emma just come out and tell McGill that she hadn't had a date in the last six months? J.D.'s last serious relationship had ended when the man insisted she sleep with him, after all the money he'd put out over the last six weeks. So she sat down, wrote him a check for five hundred dollars, then punched him in the mouth. When he threatened to press assault charges, she told him she'd stop payment on the check. She hadn't heard from him since.

She stole a glance at McGill. He had the oddest expression on his face. A cross between amusement and astonishment.

"If you filed all the depositions, you don't need to stay any longer, Emma. C'mon, McGill, we can talk in my office."

She threw her purse on the desk and dropped her shoes. As she took off her suit jacket and hung it over the desk chair, she watched him survey her office. What did he think? She worked hard to make the room welcoming. Most of her clients were poor, and she wanted an atmosphere that would make them comfortable. Her large mahogany desk gave off a warm tone, the two leather chairs in front of it were soft and roomy. Beneath the windows to one side, the overstuffed sofa with throw pillows was in pastels. The soft green carpet complemented the peach color of the walls.

She fished the two chocolate bars from her purse and held one out to him. "Want one?"

He shook his head. She moved to the couch and curled up in the corner. Eagerly, she tore into the candy bar wrapping.

"Your office is a surprise," Luke said as he sat in one of the leather chairs.

After swallowing a mouthful of chocolate, she asked, "Why do you say that?"

"The room reflects a warmth, a softness that you don't show in the courtroom."

"I'd be run over by the D.A. and the police if I wasn't tough."

"We all have our hidden sides," he mumbled. He withdrew a notebook from his inside coat pocket. Pulling out a pen, he settled back into the chair and stretched out his long legs. Her eyes were drawn to the cowboy boots he wore.

"Is that a requirement of all Dallas detectives?"

"What?"

With her candy bar, she pointed to his feet. "Is it department policy that you wear cowboy boots?"

"No, but we have discovered it makes breaking our suspects' kneecaps easier."

J.D. shot up, her feet hitting the floor. "What?"

Luke grinned. "I got you, Counselor. Who would've believed you'd be that gullible?"

"That was unfair, McGill," she said, relaxing back against the cushions.

"Maybe," he said, his voice becoming somber, "but usually people believe the worst about the police no matter how farfetched the story."

She couldn't argue. He had a point.

"How close were you to Gwen Kennedy?"

"We were friends in high school, not best friends, just friends. After we went to college, I lost track of her."

"Tell me what you know about her."

Hugging a pillow to her chest, she thought back. "Gwen and I grew up in Midland. Her dad died when she was four or five. Her mother died when Gwen was

in college. She had one brother, who left Texas when
she was in high school."

"Do you know which college she attended?"

"University of Texas, Austin campus."

"What did she do for a living?"

"I don't know."

"When you saw her last July fourth, didn't you
talk?"

"It was at a political party given by the state senator at the civic center. She and I only exchanged
greetings, then my dad pulled me away to talk to
someone else."

He frowned as if to say that didn't help this investigation. J.D. shrugged and took another bite of her
chocolate.

"So you don't have any idea why she called you?"

"She obviously was in some sort of legal trouble,
but she never said specifically what."

"Any idea where she lived?"

J.D. set down her candy and rubbed her temples,
letting her fingers trail through her hair. "No, but I
somehow got the impression she didn't live in Dallas."

"Chocolate aggravates headaches, Anderson."

She glared at him. "Thanks for the helpful information. Why didn't you say something sooner?"

"Being the chocoholic you are, I didn't think you'd
appreciate the information."

"Who says I'm a chocoholic?"

"C'mon, Anderson. Even an untrained observer
couldn't miss the stash in your purse."

"Hey, we all have our little weaknesses."

He mumbled something that sounded suspiciously
like *some more than others.*

"I didn't hear that clearly, McGill. Would you care to repeat it?"

"No, Counselor. Can you give me the name of any close friends she might have had?"

She named two of Gwen's high school friends.

"Are they still living in Midland?"

"I think so."

He clicked his pen and slipped it into his pocket. "I think that's all for now. If you can think of anything else, let me know." He laid one of his business cards on her desk.

Tossing the pillow aside, she stood. "I wish I could be of more help."

"At least we know the victim's name and where she grew up."

"What are you going to do now?"

"Run her name through DPS to see if she had a driver's license. Check the city tax roll, see if she lived here."

"Will you let me know what you find?"

"I'll try."

She grasped the rock-hard muscles of his forearm, and she felt that stupid little flutter in her stomach again. Pushing aside the sensations, she said, "I want to be kept abreast of this investigation, McGill."

He pointedly stared at her hand on his arm. Feeling foolish, she released him.

"Do you know how many investigations I've got going now? This is not TV where I can drop everything and concentrate on this case exclusively."

She held up her hands. "I know. You're understaffed and overworked. But I do have a reason for the request."

"It'd better be a beaut, Anderson."

"I think whoever killed Gwen was looking for something. She didn't have it, but they knew she'd contacted me."

"And the reason they ransacked your office was to find this evidence?"

"Yes. I think if the killer doesn't find what he wants, he'll pay me another visit."

"I think the stress of defending all those guilty clients has finally gotten to you."

"Think what you want, Detective, but I want to know what you turn up, because I think my life depends on it."

After closing the door behind Luke, J.D. rushed upstairs to her bathroom, yanked the aspirin bottle out of the medicine cabinet and swallowed the two pills without water. She should go back to her office and work, she told herself. Instead she stretched out on the bed.

Poor Gwen. Nobody should die the way she had. Gwen was so vibrant and alive last time J.D. saw her. Why did it have to end this way? Why would anyone want to kill her? What was so terrible that someone was willing to murder her to keep her silent?

Although she and Gwen hadn't been best friends in high school, J.D. remembered the quiet girl whose main ambition was to have enough money never to have to go without again. And to achieve that goal, Gwen worked hard in school and won a scholarship to college.

When J.D. saw her last July, it looked like she had made it. Gwen's clothes and jewelry had been first-class all the way. If only she'd been able to take the time to talk to her old friend, maybe the problem would've surfaced then. At least she'd have a clue to what was going on now.

With her success, had Gwen discovered the high emotional cost of wealth and decided it wasn't worth the pain money brought?

The throbbing in her head eased.

She wondered if McGill would find out anything tomorrow, and if he did, would he call her and share the information. If she knew her detective, probably not.

As her muscles relaxed and she slipped into a restless sleep, the last thing she saw was McGill's whiskey-colored eyes.

Chapter 3

J.D. hurried down the back stairs of St. Luke's Community Church to the basement, where the charity dinner and auction for the Asian community center was being held. She was late, but the circumstances had been beyond her control. Well, almost.

At the bottom step, she paused, listening. The hum of dinner chatter floated through the air. Yet it was another sound that captured her attention. A child's laughter, followed by a deep, familiar voice.

"I'm going to get you."

The child laughed again.

Before J.D. could react, a little Asian girl rounded the corner and ran into her, bouncing off her leg. In the next instant, a blindfolded Luke McGill appeared.

"I've got you." His hand shot out, catching J.D. around the hips.

The expression on his face would've been comical if the heat vibrating through her body hadn't been so devastating. For a split second, she wanted to melt into him and feel his strong arms around her.

The child's laughter brought them out of their haze. Luke whipped off the towel covering his eyes, blinking to focus. If she didn't know better, she could've sworn that Luke McGill, Supercop, was blushing. But it must have been the evening light filtering through the window above them.

"If you're here for dinner, you're late."

So much for a pleasant exchange of greetings. "My car wouldn't start."

"Figures." He held out his hands to the little girl, and she raced into his arms, screaming with delight as he tossed her into the air and caught her. "How did you get here?"

She really didn't want to admit how she'd arrived. "The bus."

A deep chuckle rumbled up from his chest. She gritted her teeth against the sensual response racing through her body. *Why, God? Of all the men on earth, why him?*

"You have a ticket for this shindig?"

"Of course," J.D. replied indignantly.

"Show me."

J.D.'s mouth dropped open. "You don't believe me? You think I'm lying?"

"I'm a cop, Counselor. I'd like to see proof."

Digging through her purse, she muttered, "I'd like to tell you what you can do with your proof."

"Tsk, tsk, and in front of this innocent child."

J.D.'s head snapped up, catching the look of wicked delight in McGill's eyes. She held the ticket under his nose. "Here."

He took the ticket from her hand. "Follow me. I'll get you something to eat." He moved across the back of the large room. Long tables had been set up and were filled with chatting people. Straight ahead she could see the kitchen through the serving counter cut into the wall.

"What are you doing here?"

"The police association supports the community center. I help where I can."

The tender picture Luke made with the tiny girl clinging to his neck, her head resting on his shoulder, forced J.D. to see him as more than a hard-nosed cop. The man standing before her was a man who cared, who could play a game of hide-and-seek blindfolded with a small child.

But what really shook J.D. was the fact that the little girl felt secure enough with Luke to seek comfort and protection from him. She recalled clearly the feel of his large hands on her hips. Suddenly the room seemed too hot, he seemed too large, and her temper too short.

Carefully, Luke set the girl on the countertop. "Don't move," he cautioned her.

"'Kay." She popped her thumb into her mouth.

"I hope you like Asian cooking," Luke said to J.D. He handed her a plate, then motioned to the row of dishes and platters on the serving counter. "The ladies in the Asian community each fixed their speciality and brought it. I can identify most of the dishes if you don't know what they are."

She smiled sourly. "Thank you, Detective."

"You're welcome, Counselor." He grinned, wagging his eyebrows at her. "C'mon, sweetheart," he said to the little girl, scooping her up. "Let's go see what's happening."

J.D. glared at his retreating back. She served herself, grabbed a cup of tea and walked back into the main room. She set her plate on the last table.

"Hello, gorgeous."

J.D. spun around and her eyes filled with delight. Instantly, she was in the man's arms. "Hello, you rascal," she said, pulling back to survey her old poker buddy. "How are you? And how's that new daughter of yours?"

Kent Bradley flashed a grin of contentment that spoke volumes about the status of his life. "I'm fine. Melody is— There aren't words to describe how great she is."

"Where's Morgan?"

"At home with the baby. Melody is cutting teeth and not in the best of moods, so Morgan decided to do everyone a favor and stay home," Kent said. "What are *you* doing here, as if I didn't know?"

J.D. shrugged. "You know me, bleeding-heart liberal, can't pass up any charity event."

Kent winked. "Sure, Ace, I believe that."

"Kent Bradley. Good to see you."

J.D. froze when she heard Luke McGill's voice.

Kent gave her a puzzled look before he turned to greet the policeman. "Hi, Luke. How have you been?"

"Fine."

"Have you met my friend J.D. Anderson?" Kent asked.

Luke nodded. "The counselor and I have crossed swords in court." His acid tone set her teeth on edge. In order to avoid saying anything, J.D. shoved a fork full of food into her mouth.

A grin broke across Kent's face. "J.D., you really must've unloaded on Luke to get such a reaction from him."

"No more so than normal," she groused.

"Shame on you, Ace, for being so merciless to the lieutenant."

"Ace?" Luke glanced from Kent to J.D., who was glaring at Kent.

"J.D. and I are old poker buddies. She worked with my wife's brother at First National Bank in Fort Worth and we used to play poker every Thursday night. J.D. was the one who got the financing for Morgan's documentary."

"Oh, that reminds me, J.D.," Kent continued. "I talked on the phone with your dad last week. He's willing to back Morgan's next project." He turned to Luke. "If it hadn't been for J.D., I don't know if Mo's film would've been made," Kent quietly added.

Luke studied J.D. She felt his surprise and knew he was dying to ask why she'd done it.

"How are the boots Martin made for you holding up?" Kent asked.

"Best I've had, Kent. They've lasted through twenty bookings and interrogations." He shot J.D. a meaningful look, reminding her of his comment about kneecaps. "I'm glad you recommended him. By the way, have you heard from him lately?"

Kent rubbed his chin thoughtfully. "No, can't say that I have."

Luke glanced at J.D., and she noticed a hesitancy in his manner as if he didn't want to say anything in front of her. "Well, maybe you can help me."

"Sure."

"Uh—I'm trying to track down a certain boot heel with the state of Texas etched into it. I thought you might know who sells such an unusual heel, since I haven't been able to get in touch with Martin."

Kent rubbed his chin. "Yeah, Martin mentioned a guy in Wichita Falls who does that fancy etching. There was such a demand for it, he quit making boots and strictly does design work."

"Is he the only one who makes them?"

"I don't know, but Martin would."

Luke mouthed an obscenity.

"Is there a problem?" Kent asked.

"No. Do you know the name of the guy in Wichita Falls?"

"Not right offhand, but I think I have his address and phone number at home."

"That's great. Would you call me tomorrow with it?"

J.D. studied McGill. He was purposely avoiding her eyes. Now, why was he doing that? Did the print of the boot heel have anything to do with Gwen's murder?

"McGill, is this boot heel connected with Gwen's case in any way?"

When he turned to her, his face was a mask of innocence. "Shh, Counselor. The auction is about to begin."

She opened her mouth to respond, but the lights in the room dimmed and the auctioneer hopped onto the stage at the front of the room.

Luke breathed a sigh of relief. He'd been saved by
the skin of his teeth and the dimming of the lights.
But, he acknowledged ruefully, it was only a temporary reprieve. J.D. wouldn't let the issue die. He hadn't
wanted to ask Kent about the boot heel in front of her,
but he knew if he'd pulled Kent to one side and quietly asked his questions, J.D. would've been instantly
suspicious. Instead, he'd gambled he could couch his
questions in broad terms, slipping it by her. No such
luck.

He shook his head. She was too damn sharp for her
own good.

He listened absentmindedly to the items auctioned
off. His mind kept replaying the moment he'd reached
out for Sue Lynn, expecting to grasp her small shoulders. Instead his hands had wrapped around slender,
womanly hips. Heat had sizzled through him. Remembering how his thumbs had rested in the hollow
next to her hipbones and his fingers had fanned out
over her rear, that heat returned full force, turning his
mood sour.

*Maybe you need a long vacation, McGill, if you get
so turned on by a set of hips.*

No, it wasn't the hips that made him a candidate for
the funny farm. It was who they belonged to.

And, of course, there was his stupid reaction to
seeing her hug Kent Bradley. When Kent returned her
hug, Luke had wanted to rush across the room and rip
the two apart. Now, what would the department psy-
chiatrist make of that?

"Next we have Detective Lucas McGill's contribu-
tion to our auction. Detective McGill has offered his
services as a handyman for this Saturday afternoon.
Any of you ladies who have a husband with ten

thumbs, or you single women who need some work done around your home by one of the finest specimens of manhood the Dallas Police Department has to offer, this is your chance.''

Luke squirmed. He wished the man would get on with it. Out of the corner of his eye, he noticed the calculating look that J.D. was giving him.

Like a bolt of lightning, the knowledge of what she was going to do hit him. He turned on her. "Don't you do it.''

Her expression was angelic, which meant he was in trouble.

"Ah, hell.''

She stood. "I bid five hundred dollars.''

All eyes turned on them. A murmur ran through the crowd.

"The bid is five hundred dollars. Are there any other bids?''

The silence was painful.

"Five hundred going once. Twice. Sold to Ms. Anderson.''

"Why did you do that?'' Luke demanded.

"This community center needs the money. I can't think of a better way to spend mine.'' She stood, a beatific smile on her face, a wicked twinkle in her eye. "Saturday, McGill. My house. Ten o'clock. Be there.''

He was dead meat.

Chapter 4

Luke pulled up in front of J.D.'s house, cut the engine, then glanced at his watch. Ten after ten. He'd driven around her neighborhood for the last few minutes to kill time, determined to show J.D. that he wasn't at her beck and call like some damn servant. He'd give her a good day's work but that's all she was going to get. Being on time wasn't included.

He wasn't in the best of moods this morning. Yesterday, a judge dismissed one of his collars and reprimanded him for the illegal search and seizure. Then a good friend on the force had been wounded in the line of duty. He'd spent half the night at the hospital with Charlie's wife, listening to her sob and complain about police work.

Now, after a short night's sleep, he was supposed to be bossed around by Counselor Anderson. He couldn't think of anything he wanted less. He was even tempted to reimburse J.D. the money she'd spent just to avoid this torture. The only problem with that scenario was that he was sure J.D. wouldn't agree to it.

With a sigh, he got out of his car and slowly walked to the house. He rang the doorbell. After a minute, he impatiently rang it again. Where was she? He was expected, so why wasn't she here? He banged on the door. "Hey, lady, you in there?"

"Do you always make such a racket?"

Luke whirled at the sound of her voice. She stood at the end of the porch, stripping off her gardening gloves and tucking them into her rear pocket. He felt himself gaping but couldn't stop. Never in his wildest dreams had he imagined J. D. Anderson dressed as she was now in a pair of tight cutoffs and a large yellow T-shirt that she'd knotted at her waist. His eyes followed her shapely legs down to the worst-looking tennis shoes he had ever seen. It amazed him that the shoes were the plain-Jane variety, the kind girls wore in the fifties and sixties. Her hair was tied back with a clip at her neck.

It was obvious she'd been working in the yard, which made him feel like a fool. "I only make a racket when I know the person's expecting me and doesn't answer."

"You sound a little cranky this morning, McGill."

He shrugged.

"Do you need coffee before you begin?" She fished a piece of paper out of the pocket of her T-shirt. Luke peeked at the paper and swallowed hard when he saw the long list.

When he didn't answer, she looked up. "You didn't answer my question. You want some coffee?"

"No, I'd rather get to what you've so carefully planned for me today."

She flashed him a self-satisfied grin. She was out for her pound of flesh and she let him know it.

"This morning I thought you could clean out the gutters for me. Then, when you finish that, you can check the roof for any loose shingles." She turned and disappeared around the side of the house.

"Is that all?" He threw the sarcastic words at her back.

She glanced over her shoulder. "No. I've got more."

"Great," he grumbled, throwing up his hands.

She walked to the detached garage that sat at the back of the property and stopped before the open door. "There's the ladder," she said, pointing out the obvious. "And the toolbox is right here," she added, pulling the red metal box from a shelf. Luke took it from her and set it on the ground.

He opened the lid and surveyed the contents. "I'm surprised that you have such a well-stocked toolbox."

"It was my father's Christmas present to me last year. He said those tools were a must for all single women."

"He's a smart man."

"Only in some areas."

Now, what was that crack supposed to mean? Before he could respond, she walked back to her garden. Luke shook his head. He wasn't here to psychoanalyze her. He was only here to work, and the sooner he started the sooner he could leave. He grabbed the ladder and headed toward the back of the house.

The day was hot, the work tedious and time-consuming. Within an hour, he'd discarded his shirt, tying it around his waist. Once he got to the driveway side of the house, he had a perfect view of J.D. on her hands and knees weeding the flower bed. He tried to ignore her, but he couldn't keep his mind on his work. What was the matter with the woman? Why couldn't she find something to do inside instead of crawling around and showing off her rear?

"You almost finished?" J.D. called to him, smashing his fantasies.

Looking down at her, he was tempted to say that things would go much faster if she took her cute little butt and went inside, but he didn't want to let her know the effect she had on him.

J.D. was having trouble of her own. She'd tried to block McGill's presence from her mind but had failed miserably. She knew he'd removed his shirt, but staring up at the broad expanse of his chest, slick from exertion, she felt her mouth go dry. What was the matter with her, acting like a thirteen-year-old girl instead of a thirty-six-year-old woman?

"Yeah, this is the last gutter I need to clean."

"Good. Then why don't we break for lunch."

His dark brow arched. "You plan on feeding me?"

She rolled her eyes. "Please, McGill, the martyr role doesn't suit you."

He shrugged, and a trickle of sweat ran down his neck. J.D.'s eyes followed the path the drop took. Her gaze jerked up, colliding with his. Her cheeks flushed.

"I figure I'll get more work out of you if I feed you and keep up your strength."

"That sounds like the lady lawyer I know."

"When you're finished, come inside."

It took him less than five minutes to finish up. He scrambled down the ladder, leaving it in place for the next task.

As he stepped into the kitchen, the air-conditioning surrounded him. "Ah, that feels good," he murmured with sensual abandon.

Thundering silence followed his declaration. *Say something, fool,* Luke told himself. "Where's your bathroom so I can wash up?"

"Straight ahead," J.D. said.

It took a moment for his eyes to adjust to the dimness of the room. The last thing he wanted to do was walk into the wall or stumble over a chair and further humiliate himself.

"While you're in there," she said over her shoulder, "take a look at the sink faucet. It needs to be replaced and it's on your list."

"You missed your calling in life, lady," he responded. "You should've been a slave driver."

Her low chuckle followed him into the bathroom. After scrubbing his hands and arms up to the elbows, he dunked his head under the cool flow of water. Catching sight of himself in the mirror, he finger-combed his hair. He looked like he'd come off a two-day drunk. Too bad. He slipped on his shirt. If the lady didn't like how he looked, she could eat by herself.

When he came back into the kitchen, he glanced at the table and frowned when he saw only two glasses of ice tea.

"Don't worry, McGill, you've been saved from my tuna-salad sandwiches."

"You call a pizza place or something?"

"No, my neighbor saw us in the yard and took pity on us."

"J.D., are you in there?" The call came from the driveway.

"In here, Sarah." J.D. moved to the door and held it open. "Do you need any help?"

"No, everything's under control."

Luke immediately recognized the plump brunette as the same woman who'd been hovering around J.D. the night of the break-in. In one hand she held a covered basket, in the other some sort of pot with a wire handle.

"Sarah, you remember meeting Detective McGill."

The woman set her things on the table and offered Luke her hand. "It's nice to see you, Detective, under more pleasant circumstances."

Luke nodded.

"Sarah, you really didn't have to do this," J.D. said. She lifted the lid on the pot and took a deep breath of the fragrant homemade soup.

"Yes, I did. Larry just raved and raved about the dinner you cooked for us last night. And that cake, o-o-oh, it was so-o-o good." She turned to Luke. "It was called Death by Chocolate." With a dramatic sigh, she said, "It was heavenly."

"Still, you didn't have to do this, but I'm glad you did." J.D.'s hand swept the table.

"It's nothing. It was already made. Larry couldn't come home for lunch, and when I saw you two working so hard—" She shrugged. "I'm glad my efforts won't be wasted." She bounced out of the kitchen. "Enjoy," she called, descending the outside steps.

Luke flopped down in a kitchen chair. So J.D. could cook. It figured. *Ms. Perfection* didn't seem to have any faults, which irritated him no end. Why couldn't she be like most career-minded women, not worth spit in the kitchen? His ex-wife had been a good cook at one time, but once she'd been bitten by the success bug, she didn't give a tinker's damn about fixing meals for him. She usually slapped a cold sandwich before him or told him to go out and get something to eat.

"I assure you Sarah's a wonderful cook."

Disgruntled, Luke glanced up. "I didn't say she wasn't."

"From the look on your face, you could've fooled me." J.D. pulled bowls and spoons from the hutch by the table.

"I'm sorry if my expression offends you."

She ladled out the soup and handed him a bowl. "It's not that, McGill. I was just curious about the sour expression on your face."

"Do you really want to know?" He pulled the napkin off the basket and, seeing steaming pieces of corn bread, helped himself to a large chunk.

"Yes."

"I was thinking about how you're a typical career woman, and they usually don't have time to cook."

"Where does this wonderful insight of yours spring from, Detective?" she asked as she sat down.

When she called him "Detective" it was a sure sign she was irritated with him. "I was married to one. Although she knew how to cook, she couldn't be bothered. Cooking for her husband wasn't a high priority on her list. It didn't help her get ahead in the corporate world."

He didn't look at her, but busied himself with his minestrone soup. Why on earth had he told her that? He braced himself for a comeback. He'd shown her a weakness and the killer instinct she possessed in court would come to her aid now. He might as well give a criminal his gun and tell him to shoot. The results would probably be the same.

But she said nothing. Instead she quietly sipped her soup.

He leaned back in his chair. He wanted to know why she didn't jump on the opening, but he was grateful she hadn't.

"So you baked a cake called Death by Chocolate? Sounds like something you'd make."

She lifted one shoulder. "Well, you know how I am about chocolate."

"Too bad you don't have any left. I'd like to taste it."

With a conspiratorial smile, she rose and moved across the kitchen. From the back of a cupboard, she pulled a foil-wrapped plate. Bringing it to the table, she whipped off the aluminum. Two pieces of the most sinful, mouth-watering cake he'd ever seen lay on the plate.

"I was saving this—"

Luke laughed. "You mean you were hoarding it."

J.D. tried to suppress a chuckle but failed. "You're right. If Sarah's husband ever saw this, it'd be gone in a second."

She retrieved two forks from the drawer and held them up. "Want to join me?"

"That's the best offer I've had all week," he answered, taking the fork.

They made quick work of the two pieces of cake. Luke couldn't decide if it was the pure sensual pleasure of the rich chocolate cake or the intimacy of eating from the same plate, but something shifted deep inside him. A loosening.

And it scared him.

He glanced at J.D. to see if she noticed anything strange about him, but she was lost in her own world of delight.

J.D. sat quietly in the kitchen chair and listened to Luke climb up onto her roof. She was still feeling shaky from the unexpected closeness that had developed between Luke and her during lunch. When the information about his wife slipped out, she hadn't had the heart to take advantage of his vulnerability. Instead, she had wanted to reach out and cover his hand with hers and tell him that she could identify with his hurt. It matched her own. Wisely, she had refrained.

But what had truly shaken her was the sensual abandon they'd shared as they ate the cake. It went beyond taste and smell. It moved into the realm of mutual pleasure, a single intense moment of sheer ecstasy experienced by two people, almost like two lovers who—

She jumped to her feet and gathered the dishes. It wasn't a smart idea to pursue that line of thought. It would only bring trouble.

Besides, what did she know? Her marriage didn't make her an expert on mutual pleasure.

The afternoon passed quickly for Luke. He hammered down the loose shingles, replaced the downstairs bathroom faucet, then installed a new shower head in her upstairs bathroom. He felt uncomfortable surrounded by her things, the flowers on the vanity, the basket of sweet-smelling soaps on the tank of the commode, the lacy, ribboned hand towel hanging from the rack.

"Can I help?" J.D. strolled into the room.

Luke glanced over his shoulder. "Nope. Got everything under control."

J.D. leaned against the doorjamb and crossed her arms. "McGill, answer a question for me."

"Sure, what is it?"

"Did that boot heel with the outline of Texas on it have anything to do with Gwen's murder?"

The wrench he was using to tighten the last nut on the shower arm slipped, and he cracked the knuckles of his other hand.

"Damn," he growled, shaking his bruised hand.

"Is that comment in response to the pain or to my question?"

He threw her a dark look.

"I bet you thought I forgot about it."

"I couldn't be that lucky," he grumbled.

"Does it have anything to do with her murder?"

"Why would you think that? You yourself commented that most of the detectives on the force wear Western boots. I was just inquiring about an unusual pair."

"That's not an answer."

He finished tightening the nut, picked up his tools and the old shower head, and nudged past her as he left the bathroom. "What do you want to do with this old thing?" he asked, holding up the dented shower head.

She grabbed it from his hand and tossed it onto the floor. "You didn't answer my question."

"What do you want me to do next?" he asked, walking out of her bedroom. Not for all the tea in China was he going to stop and argue in her bedroom.

J.D. planted her hands on her hips. "McGill."

Once in the hall, he stopped and turned. "Counselor, you paid for my manual labor and that's all. I'm not obligated to answer any questions. Now, if you don't have anything else for me to do, I'll leave."

"No, you don't," she said, darting out of the room after him. "There's still one more thing I need you to help me do."

He didn't like the sound of that. "Oh?" He raised his brow.

She pointed to the ceiling. "I've got an attic that needs work."

Luke groaned. "You're going to get your money's worth, aren't you?"

"You bet. If my daddy taught me anything, it was how to get the most out of my investment."

"Remind me to have a long talk with your old man."

With a smug smile she showed him the way to the attic.

"C'mon, McGill, this is the last thing we have to take downstairs."

Luke eyed the old steamer trunk. For an hour and a half they'd been wading through the debris left behind by the previous owners. After countless trips to the backyard with a fifty-gallon garbage can full of trash, this battered trunk was the only thing that stood between him and freedom.

He studied the trunk, then J.D. "I'll need help in hauling this thing downstairs. You think you're up to it?"

She looked around the attic. "I'm the only one here, and I want to get rid of this thing." She rubbed her hands together. "Let's do it."

There was a nagging doubt in the back of Luke's mind, but he pushed it aside. He grabbed the leather handle on one end and J.D. got the other.

"Let me go first," he said. "That way, I'll take most of the weight of the trunk."

J.D. was on the first step. "Don't worry about it, McGill. I can handle it."

She did—for all of seven steps. J.D. missed the last tread, lost her hold and tumbled to the second-floor hall. Cursing, Luke braced the trunk on his knees and wrestled it to the floor.

"Sorry about that." J.D. jumped up and brushed off the back of her cutoffs.

"You okay?" he asked.

"Yes."

He carefully studied her. "You sure? You look a little strange."

"That's plain embarrassment, McGill. Nothing more. I'm fine. Now, why don't we get this trunk downstairs?"

It was clear she didn't want any sympathy. But more than that, it was as if she were going to show him that if he could do this, she could. She wouldn't quit.

After wiping her hands on the seat of her shorts, she grasped the trunk handle again. He put his hands on her shoulders and moved her aside. Her eyes flared with fire, but before she could spit out any of the flames, he said, "I'll take this end."

Immediately, the fire in her died down. She nodded and walked to the other end of the trunk.

"On the count of three we'll lift."

J.D. felt like an idiot for missing that step. She knew she was touchy about what happened, but she didn't want to fail in front of McGill. He was like her fa-

ther. Hard, driving, expecting the best from himself
and those around him. And, of course, when those
mere humans around him failed, he didn't understand. Instead he would interpret it as a sign of weakness. Well, she refused to let McGill think her weak.

As they moved down the stairs, J.D. felt her hands
begin to cramp. If she could just hold on a few more
minutes, she'd have it made.

"Are you okay?" Luke asked. "Do we need to stop
and rest?"

She shook her head. "No. Let's just get this over."

He hesitated, shrugged and moved down another
step. J.D. looked over his shoulder. Five more steps,
a small landing, then the stairs made a ninety-degree
turn, then there were four more treads.

Her hands were beginning to lose their grip. Luke
went down another step and the leather handle slipped
out of her fingers.

Luke yelled and tumbled backwards. The momentum of the trunk sent him crashing into the railing on
the landing. He staggered sideways and fell down the
rest of the stairs.

J.D. stared in horror for a moment, then rushed
down after him. As she skirted the trunk, her toe
caught the corner and she pitched forward, tumbling
down the last few stairs and landing on Luke. He
grunted.

With the wind knocked out of her, it took a moment for her to catch her breath. Slowly, she raised her
head and met his gaze. Luke looked like a landed fish,
eyes dazed, mouth open.

The humor of the situation hit her. The corners of
her mouth twitched, but the harder she tried to suppress the urge to laugh, the harder it became.

A half-choked giggle escaped, and she held her breath, afraid Luke wouldn't appreciate her sense of humor. Instead, he broke out into laughter, joining her.

"We're a pair," he gasped, his hands settling around her waist.

"I haven't seen anything that funny since the *Pink Panther*," J.D. said, resting her hands on his shoulders.

Luke rolled and pinned J.D. under him. "Are you saying I remind you of Peter Sellers?"

J.D. arched her brow. "If the shoe fits..."

"You're going to take that back, Counselor."

"Make me."

The challenge hung in the air between them.

"You shouldn't have said that." His tone was light, full of humor, his eyes dancing with mischief.

"I'm shaking in my boots, McGill."

Immediately Luke's hands were at her waist and he began to tickle her.

"Unfair," she gasped between laughs. She tried to bat his hands away. He caught her wrists and pinned them by her head.

Their laughter died slowly. In its place came an awareness of the intimate way their bodies touched. With each deep breath, J.D. felt Luke's body, every manly inch of him, pressed against hers.

Her eyes locked with his. The dark fire burning in his gaze pulled her toward him. As insane as it was, she wanted his kiss.

Luke's mouth covered hers with a sweet violence that shook her to her core. Instead of retreating from his aggressive lips, she returned his kiss with equal fervor.

The feelings rocketing through her felt right. She moaned, allowing Luke to deepen their kiss.

Fire enveloped J.D. and she buried her hands in his hair, wanting an anchor in her swiftly changing world.

"Am I interrupting?"

The words smashed their private universe. Before J.D. could pull her scattered thoughts together, Luke rolled to his side and stood.

"And just who are you to come barging in here?" Luke demanded, confronting the older man.

"I'm this little lady's daddy. Who the hell are you?"

Chapter 5

Luke glanced down at J.D. "Is this man your father?"

The one moment of her life when she had experienced complete abandon and wanted privacy had to be witnessed by her father.

She scrambled to her feet. "Don't you believe in knocking, Dad?"

"I did. Nearly put my fist through the door, girl." George Anderson turned to Luke. "Who are you?"

"Luke McGill."

"You want to explain what I just saw?" George demanded like some father from a Victorian novel.

J.D. saw red. She didn't want her father acting as if her virtue had been compromised. Besides, he had no business preaching morality to her with *his* track record. Hands on her hips, she glared at him. "That's none of your business. I'm old enough not to have to explain my actions to you."

"I was just trying to protect you," George groused.

"I don't need your protection," she shot back. "And I certainly don't need you going around acting like an outraged father. You taught me how to fend for myself. Are you questioning the job you did?"

"I wasn't questioning your ability. I was just questioning this man's motives." He jabbed his forefinger in Luke's direction.

J.D.'s chin went up a notch. "And you don't think I can see through the false lines men put out?"

George said nothing, but his silence was a painful reminder of the one time she had not.

"Hey, if anyone around here needs protecting, it's me," Luke said, breaking the tense scene. He pointed to the trunk. "First she tries to kill me with that thing. Then, when that doesn't work, she tries a flying tackle. I'm lucky if I don't have any broken ribs." He turned to J.D. "And if I do, I think I'll sue."

It took her a moment to realize that Luke was teasing. After her shock wore off, she chuckled. "Try, McGill, and I'll slaughter you in court."

"It wouldn't be the first time," he muttered under his breath.

George leaned forward. "What did you say?"

Luke clamped his mouth shut.

"He's just complaining that I've beat him before in court."

"You're a lawyer?" George said it with such horror and distaste that Luke and J.D. laughed.

"No. I haven't sunk that low."

George breathed a sigh of relief. "Then what do you do, McGill?"

"I'm a detective with the Dallas Police Department."

George nodded his head. "Well, well, the girl's finally showing some sense."

Before her father could say anything else that might embarrass her, J.D. asked, "Dad, what are you doing in Dallas?"

"Well, I'm flying to Venezuela later tonight to negotiate an oil deal, and since I was in town, I thought I'd take you to dinner. Of course, your friend here is welcome to join us."

"I'm not really dressed for dinner out," Luke said, looking down at his dusty jeans and shirt.

"Nonsense, Luke. We'll go somewhere informal. How about that Mexican restaurant over on Knox, Juliet Desiree? Aren't they casual over there?"

Luke's eyes widened and his jaw dropped. He looked at J.D. and mouthed her full name.

Her eyes burning with wrath, J.D. dared him to say her name out loud. *Do it, McGill, and those will be the last words out of your mouth.*

"Yeah, Dad, that's the one," she absently answered, still glowering at Luke.

"Then we'll all go there. I've got a rental car out front, so we don't have to take that piece of junk you drive."

Still reeling from shock, embarrassment and the strange feelings Luke's kiss had produced, she wanted a moment to gather herself before having to endure both her father and Luke for the balance of the evening.

"Let me lock up and get my purse. I'll meet you out front." As she passed Luke, she whispered, "If anyone ever finds out what my name is, I'll kill you."

It took less than fifteen minutes to drive from J.D.'s house on Swiss to the restaurant on Knox. It wasn't crowded this early in the evening and they were immediately escorted to a table. Luke didn't bother with the menu, since he already knew what he wanted to order. Instead, he studied J.D. She'd been unusually quiet on the drive over. She was wearing her courtroom mask, letting no one see beyond the surface layer of her emotions.

So much had happened this afternoon that he felt punch-drunk. First she tried to work him to death. Then she tried to kill him with that trunk.

His eyes were drawn to her mouth and he remembered the incredible kiss they had shared. He could still taste her sweetness now and wanted to grab her hand, drag her from the restaurant and find the nearest bed.

"What are you going to have, Luke?" George—her father, the man who'd found him on the floor with her—asked.

Luke wanted to knock himself in the head. What was the matter with him, lusting at J.D. like that in front of her father? Maybe that tumble down the stairs had loosened a few screws.

"Luke?"

"The fajitas."

"What about you, Juliet Desiree?"

Luke watched her mouth tighten. He couldn't blame her. When her father had called her that the first time, Luke had felt like he'd been hit in the back of the head with a two-by-four. Juliet Desiree? What kind of name was that, especially for J.D.?

"I'll have a salad."

"Honey, you need more than that. How about—"

"I don't want anything else." She said the words quietly, with a strength and dignity that brooked no argument.

George shrugged, then motioned for the waiter to take their order. Luke leaned back in his chair, amazed at the scene he'd just witnessed. J.D. couldn't stand her name, but she put up no fight when her father called her by it. Yet, when George would've pushed her to order something else, she put her foot down, and the maverick oilman honored her decision.

After they ordered, George turned to J.D. "When I was at the state capitol a couple of weeks ago, I saw Allen."

Luke couldn't believe his eyes. J.D. turned a slight color of green.

"That's nice," she murmured around a corn chip.

George gave a short laugh. "He had the nerve to come up to me and say hello. I told him what he could do with his hello."

The comment brought life to J.D.'s eyes and the corners of her mouth lifted. "What did he say to that?"

"Since we were outside the senate chamber, surrounded by dozens of people, there wasn't much he could say without revealing what a bastard he really is."

"It couldn't have happened to a nicer guy," J.D. said.

George leaned toward Luke. "Allen Danford used to be married to Juliet Desiree, until she wised up and divorced him."

Why was George Anderson bothering to explain who Allen was to him? Luke began to squirm. He hoped the older man hadn't read more into that little

incident with him and J.D. on the floor in the throes
of a passionate embrace than there really was.

And what was there? he asked himself.

"Dad, I'm sure Detective McGill doesn't want a
detailed history of my life." She was back to her cold
court voice, but he saw a touch of panic in her eyes.

"I just want the boy prepared for what he's getting."

"Dad—"

"And why do you call him Detective McGill? After
what I saw, you should at least call him Luke."

The waiter appeared with their food, postponing
further discussion. When he left the table, George
plunged on. "Did Gwen Kennedy ever get in contact
with you?"

Both J.D. and Luke froze. She glanced at him, then
her father. "You talked to Gwen? When? Where?"

"Whoa, girl," George said, holding up his hand.
"Slow down. Let's see." He rubbed his chin. "Why,
it was on that same trip when I saw Allen. I ran into
Gwen as I was leaving the capitol building. She
stopped me, asked if you were still practicing law.
Asked what kind of law you specialized in. I gave her
your address and phone number."

"Did you hear that, Luke?" Excitement throbbed
in her voice. "Gwen probably lived in Austin. Maybe
she had a job with the state? Isn't that great?"

Luke didn't look surprised. His lack of enthusiasm
puzzled her.

"I take it she called you?" George asked J.D.

"Yes." She tried to meet Luke's eyes, but he refused to look at her. "She told me she was in trouble
and arranged to meet me. She never made the meeting. She was murdered after she called."

George's eyes widened. "What? Murdered? I can't believe it. Who'd want to kill that lovely lady?" His bushy brows puckered into a deep frown, and he turned to Luke. "Do you think her murder was connected with her contacting J.D?"

Luke answered. "Yes, we do."

George speared Luke with a steely gaze. "Well, what are the police doing about it?"

"Investigating it," Luke calmly replied. "And right now, you're a good lead. What else do you know about Gwen Kennedy? Do you know what she did for a living or who her friends were?"

George's expression softened. Apparently, he was satisfied with Luke's response. "No. That was the first time I'd seen her in ten years."

J.D. studied Luke. Why had he taken the news about Gwen so coolly, almost as if he already knew she'd lived in Austin? Her eyes widened and her hand convulsed around her fork. He knew. The louse knew Gwen's address and hadn't told her as he'd promised.

It was the last straw. The turmoil of the kiss, her father's sudden appearance, the embarrassment of Luke hearing about her ex-husband. And now, his betrayal.

Her rage spread outward from the burning center of her soul. She began to shake, and J.D. knew if she didn't leave the table this instant, she was going to do and say things that would be talked about in Dallas for years to come.

"Excuse me." She stood, grabbed her purse and walked away.

Luke watched her stop the hostess and ask a question.

"Don't worry about her," George said. "She's probably asking where the ladies' room is."

Luke had an uneasy feeling but didn't voice his doubt.

"You'll have to excuse Juliet's reaction. She's kinda touchy about her divorce."

"I can understand her feelings."

"I was amazed she stayed with that jerk as long as she did. But then again, maybe I do understand why she tried for so long."

George leaned forward, and Luke knew he wasn't going to like what the older man was about to say. "I'll let you in on a little secret. I know the reason Juliet wouldn't give up on Allen for so long. She didn't want to admit she could make the same mistake I did."

Luke silently groaned.

"You see, when Juliet was twelve, I got a divorce from her mother. Well, in a town the size of Midland, my divorce from one of the daughters of the old guard was a big item in the media. Carol, my first wife, didn't handle it very well and began to drink. That devastated Juliet. Carol was killed a couple of years later in a car accident. She was drunk. Juliet was in the car with her."

Stop! I don't want to hear any more, Luke wanted to yell at George. *Don't tell me about J.D.'s problems. I don't want to know. I don't want to see her as a vulnerable woman who's been hurt by the men in her life. I want to see her as the enemy.*

Luke didn't want to foul up his dislike of J.D. with any intimate knowledge or understanding or sympathy. She would still tear a strip off him in court, given the opportunity.

He rubbed his aching head. It was hard to think straight with his hormones still running amok from the kiss they shared.

"I'll tell you this, Luke. Something happened between Juliet and Allen. She never told me, but when she filed for divorce, Allen quietly slipped from the picture, instead of petitioning for the big bucks he could've got out of me via my daughter. Makes me wonder. 'Course, Juliet was never the same after that. It was like something died in that girl. She turned cold toward men and buried herself in that peculiar practice of hers."

Warning shouts sounded in Luke's head. Daddy here was looking for husband number two for his darling daughter and apparently thought he, Luke McGill, was a good candidate. He raised his wrist to glance at his watch. "Hasn't J.D. been gone for a long time?"

George's brows wrinkled. "She sure has." He motioned for the hostess.

"May I help you, sir?" she asked, stopping by the table.

"The young lady who was seated with us has been gone a long time. Would you check the bathroom and make sure she's okay?"

"That won't be necessary, sir. The lady had me call a cab. She left about ten minutes ago."

"Left?" George blurted.

"Yes, sir. But she left a message for you gentlemen."

"Well, what was it?"

"'Bye, Dad. McGill, drop dead.'" The girl flushed. "Those were her exact words," she hastily added.

Throwing back his head, George roared with laughter. He patted Luke on the back. "Well, I told you she was touchy about her divorce. Serves me right for saying anything within earshot of her." George threw down several bills. "You need a ride back to the house?"

Luke had the suspicion that J.D. wasn't as put out about her divorce as her father thought. It was something else that upset her. Something like him knowing Gwen's address and not telling her. When he saw her again, there would be hell to pay.

Through the window, Luke saw his salvation. A patrol car was stopped at the intersection and he wouldn't be forced to hear any more of J.D.'s personal life. "I'll catch a ride. Good luck with your trip."

"Well, since you've got a ride, I'll just head on out to the airport. No need to bother Juliet right now. Tell her I'll see her when I get back."

Luke had the strangest feeling that George didn't want to face his daughter. Interesting.

Running outside, Luke flagged down the officer in the car. "Gary, can you give me a ride over to Swiss to get my car?"

"Sure, Luke. What's your car doing over there?"

"I left it there when I went to dinner."

"That wasn't a smart move. The trouble we've been having over there, it might not be in one piece when you get back."

"That's not what I'm worried about. I left it parked in front of J.D. Anderson's house. She's angry with me, and I'm afraid she just might set the thing on fire."

Gary glanced at him, then chuckled. "I wouldn't put it past her."

"Yeah, I know. And that's what worries me."

Luke breathed a sigh of relief when he spotted his car intact, but his relief didn't last long. As they pulled up in front of J.D.'s home, they heard a shot. Instantly Luke was out of the car, running toward the side door, followed by the patrolman.

"Take the front door," Luke yelled over his shoulder.

A moment later, two men tumbled out the side door, cursing and looking worse for wear.

"Stop," Luke ordered. "Police."

Startled, they faced Luke.

"Run," the taller suspect yelled at his partner. He raised his right hand, and Luke saw the gun in time to duck. The man fired once, then turned to follow the other man down the alley.

"Luke, you all right?" Gary called from his position.

"Fine." He didn't give a second thought to the suspects. J.D. was inside and he needed to find her. Fear, like nothing he'd ever known, wrapped itself around his heart. She had to be all right.

He moved through the kitchen and down the hall, prepared to disarm anyone else who might be lurking in the shadows. A soft moan came from the room directly before him. He glanced around the doorway and spotted J.D. in the corner, slumped against the metal filing cabinet.

In three steps he was at her side. "J.D., are you hurt?" Kneeling before her, he helped her settle back against the wall. He ran his hands over her face and through her hair, checking for cuts and lumps.

"What are you doing?" she asked, batting away his hands.

"Checking for injuries." He continued his inspection, feeling her arms and legs.

"Stop it, Luke. I'm fine. I was only momentarily stunned when that creep knocked me into the cabinet."

"Luke, they got away," Gary announced as he entered the room.

J.D. looked up at the uniformed patrolman. "My, Dallas's finest are on their toes today."

"Gary drove me here from the restaurant. Aren't you lucky?"

"Too bad you weren't here ten minutes ago, when I walked in on those two."

"If you hadn't stomped off like you did, I would've been here with you."

J.D. leaned forward. "So it's my fault that you're a lying snake? You knew where Gwen lived and didn't tell me."

Luke threw up his hands.

She glanced around. "Where's my dad?"

"He decided not to face the tiger he baited. He's on his way to the airport."

"Just what's that crack supposed to mean?"

"Whoa, you two." Gary stepped into the fray. "If you'll recall, we've got a crime here. Could I get some information from the victim?"

Luke stood and moved across the room, his back to her. His heart was still thudding and the taste of fear was sour on his tongue. He heard the rustling of cloth and J.D.'s moan.

"Here, let me help you to the couch," Gary told her. "Can you give me a description of the two men?"

"They were in their twenties. Both had brown hair. They were in jeans and dark T-shirts. There's a bullet in that wall over there." She pointed. "Maybe that'll help."

Luke held out his hand and watched it tremble. He wrapped it around his middle.

"No distinguishing marks?"

"No, but one of the men shouldn't be hard to find."

"Oh? Why is that?"

"I bit him on the wrist. Right wrist. I lost my hold on him when he backhanded me into the filing cabinet."

Gary's eyes widened. "Are you kidding me?" He turned toward Luke. "Is she kidding me?"

Luke glanced over his shoulder. "No," he said, his voice deadly calm. "If she said she bit him, she did." Luke was torn between shaking J.D. until her teeth rattled, and holding her and giving her the comfort and protection she'd never gotten from the males in her life.

Shaking his head, Gary said, "I'll call in these descriptions."

Luke waited until Gary was out of the house. He turned and pinned J.D. with his eyes. "Who do you think you are? Some kind of super woman?"

Her spine straightened. "I beg your pardon?"

"You ought to do a hell of a lot more than that. That was a stupid thing you did, lady. Those creeps could've seriously hurt you." He didn't understand the anger that was raging through him.

"I can take care of myself, Detective. I've got a brown belt in judo."

"Oh, a lot of good it does against a bullet." With each word, he took a step toward her. "I've seen cops, good men, trained to defend themselves, experts at a dozen martial arts, die with one bullet." He towered over her, shaking with his wrath like some vengeful god.

She couldn't keep eye contact with him and looked down at the sofa cushion. "McGill, I haven't gone looking for trouble. It's found me. And since the Dallas Police Department doesn't seem to want to help—" she pointedly looked at him "—I'm going to try, to the best of my ability, to protect myself. And the only way I can see to do that is discover who killed Gwen."

"How do you know these break-ins are connected with Gwen's murder?"

"Give me a break, McGill. It's obvious the killer thinks Gwen gave me some sort of damning evidence. This guy will try again, so before he gets me, I plan to nab him."

"And just how do you plan to do that?"

"I'm flying to Austin tomorrow, and the first thing I'm going to do is open the phone directory and look for Gwen's address. Then I'm going to the capitol building and start asking questions, sticky questions, and see how many toes I can step on until something shakes loose."

The woman was a pain—a royal pain—but she had a point. He didn't think the break-ins would stop until the killer got what he wanted. "You won't find many people in their offices on Sunday."

Her blue eyes turned nearly black with her anger. "I'll stay until I get answers," she said through clenched teeth.

The lady was a formidable force, and he'd rather have her working with him than against him. "Why don't you come with me on Monday."

"Why would I want to do that?"

"Because the authorities will be more inclined to cooperate with me than they would with a loose cannon like you."

She looked like she wanted to kick him. "All right, McGill. I'll go with you on Monday. But if I find out that you've been holding out on me about anything on this case, the deal's off."

The nightmare woke J.D. Her skin was wet with perspiration, her heart racing. She'd dreamed the men had broken into her house again. This time they held a knife to her throat, demanding to know where the evidence Gwen had given her was hidden. Luke had barged into the room, his gun drawn, his eyes wild with rage. When the man with the knife told Luke to throw down his gun or he would cut her throat, Luke did.

She woke, stunned at McGill's actions. Throwing back the covers, she slipped from the bed. The long lace-and-satin gown flowed around her legs as she walked across the room. Wouldn't Luke and his cronies in the department be surprised if they saw her in this nightgown from the lingerie shop? They probably thought she went to bed in iron sheeting.

J.D. froze. What was she thinking? And when had she started thinking of Detective McGill as Luke? Suddenly she felt the need for a chocolate fix. Pulling her purse from the corner chair, she pawed through it, looking for a candy bar.

Nothing.

She turned it over and shook out the contents on the bureau. Three wrappers but no candy. Then she remembered the bag of candy-coated chocolates stashed in the kitchen.

She padded downstairs and, in the dark, forgot about the trunk on the landing. Her left foot caught the corner of the monstrosity.

"McGill, this is your fault," she grumbled, holding on to the banister, waiting for the pain to pass. She hobbled to the kitchen, snatched the large bag from the pantry and ripped it open.

What was the matter with her to let a dream rattle her? she wondered, munching on a handful of chocolates.

"It wasn't the dream," she argued to the empty room. "It was Luke's behavior. I never thought he'd surrender his weapon—even in my imagination."

She threw another candy into her mouth. As a matter of fact, Luke's behavior last evening was even more puzzling. Why had he been so angry? His attitude reminded her of her dad's the time their house in Midland had been broken into—outraged that anyone dared endanger his loved ones.

She shook her head. That couldn't possibly be right. Luke had no feelings for her except disdain for the people she defended. No, she had to take that back. After their impassioned kiss this afternoon, she definitely knew Luke McGill had other feelings for her. But lust had nothing to do with caring. So why had he been so mad?

She plucked a green candy from the bag and popped it into her mouth. Something else was bothering her. Luke's easy capitulation over the issue of her going to Austin. Why hadn't he argued harder against her going? Why had he offered to let her accompany him? Had he finally realized that she was right and the break-ins were connected with Gwen?

No.

Funny, now that he had changed his mind, she discovered she really didn't want to be within a hundred yards of Luke McGill for any reason. He stirred too many painful emotions she thought she'd buried when she divorced Allen. She didn't want any part of the roller-coaster ride that those feelings brought.

And if she wasn't around Luke, then those twinges would never have a chance to come to life again. She was tempted to call him and tell him she wasn't going on Monday.

"That's the coward's way out, Anderson, and you can't do that. If you can stand your ground with your father, you certainly can take on one measly police detective with one hand tied behind your back."

Sure you can, a little voice mocked. *Just as long as McGill keeps his hands and kisses to himself.*

Chapter 6

Luke enjoyed flying. He liked viewing the world from thirty thousand feet, where everything seemed beautiful and perfect. Why, even the part of West Texas he was from seemed like a wonderland from the sky.

The normal glitches that bothered other passengers didn't bother him—that is, until today.

The small space the airline crammed three people into seemed to have shrunk since the last time he flew. Every time J.D. turned a page of her magazine, her arm brushed his. Each time she crossed her legs—which she could do without any trouble, he noted sourly—and wiggled her hips, he felt it.

He tried to ignore her by reading the airline magazine in the pocket in front of him, but suddenly all he could think of was how good she smelled. And how much he wanted to lean over and kiss that spot right behind her ear.

He didn't know what insanity had seized him last Saturday, but kissing J.D. was one of the biggest mistakes of his life. It was one thing to lust after a woman from a distance, never quite knowing what you were missing. It was something else to have tasted that forbidden fruit and be left wanting. Before, he'd been able to rein in his fantasies. Now, his imagination ran wild, with no restraints and plenty of sensations to build on. He hadn't had a decent night's sleep since.

"Are you finished with your drink?" the flight attendant asked J.D.

"Yes," J.D. replied, leaning across him to pass her cup to the stewardess. Her breast brushed against Luke's chest. His eyes drifted closed and his teeth clenched to keep back the scream tearing at his throat.

Forty minutes—that's how long the flight from Dallas to Austin took—sitting next to her, and he was reduced to a sniveling idiot with his hormones raging out of control.

His mood was rotten by the time the plane touched down in Austin.

Without a word to J.D., he rented a car and drove them to the Austin address on Gwen's driver's licence. The exclusive apartment building looked out over Townlake. Only the rich and powerful lived at this address. A security guard in the lobby stopped them.

"You can't get on the elevators unless you're a listed guest on my sheet," the man said.

J.D. felt anger radiating off Luke, like heat from a stove. He reached inside his sports coat and pulled out his badge.

"I'm with the Dallas Police Department, investigating the murder of one of your residents. I'd like to speak with the manager of this building."

The guard picked up his phone and within two minutes a slender man appeared in the lobby.

"I'm Donald Hays. May I help you, Detective McGill?"

"I'd like to see Gwen Kennedy's apartment."

"Do you have a search warrant?"

"No," Luke said, "but I can get one if I have to."

"Well, go ahead if you want, but it still won't do you any good."

"And why is that?" Luke's harsh tone caused the security guard to visibly flinch. But not the apartment manager. Luke bristled.

"Because," Mr. Hays said with an air of authority, "Ms. Kennedy moved out about three weeks ago."

Luke rubbed the back of his neck. "Do you have a forwarding address?"

"Yes."

"Would you mind getting me the new address, or do I need to call the Austin police to obtain your cooperation?"

"Wait here," the man curtly ordered.

Luke whirled around and mumbled something under his breath about the man's parentage. J.D. turned her head to hide her smile.

"Was Gwen really murdered?" the security guard asked J.D.

"Unfortunately, yes."

He shook his head. "I can't imagine anyone hurting her. She was such a nice girl. Of course, I didn't understand when she split up with Mr. Weston. They were such a perfect couple." He leaned forward and added with a conspiratorial whisper, "If you ask me, Ms. Kennedy should've made him move out, instead of the other way around."

"You mean Gwen was living with a man, and he's still here in this building?"

"Yes, ma'am."

J.D. glanced over at Luke. He was staring out the glass doors, rocking back on his heels. If she called him over here to further question the security guard, she had the feeling the older man would clam up. "What's Mr. Weston's full name?"

"Hal Weston."

"Do you know what he did for a living?"

"Yeah. He's the co-owner of a PR firm, Weston & Odell, over on Congress Avenue."

J.D. winked at the man. "Thanks. You've been a big help."

"You won't tell Hays I told you anything?"

"It will be our little secret."

Donald Hays reappeared in the lobby. "Here it is," he said, handing Luke a piece of paper. "If you want anything else, get a court order."

Luke slipped the paper into his coat pocket. "I'd be careful if I were you, Mr. Hays. A person with an attitude like yours makes lots of enemies and few friends."

"Are you threatening me, Detective?"

"Of course not, Mr. Hays. Why, the good counselor here would report me to the ACLU and hang my hide out to dry. Isn't that so, J.D.?"

She didn't bother answering Luke. "Thank you for your cooperation, Mr. Hays," J.D. smoothly said, taking Luke's arm and leading him to the door.

Hays glared at them until they left the building.

Luke slammed the car door closed and shoved the key into the ignition. "I'd like about five minutes alone with Mr. Hays."

J.D. shook her head. "You amaze me, McGill."

"Why is that?" He pointed to the glove compartment. "Hand me the city map."

She retrieved it and gave it to him. He pulled Gwen's address from his pocket and checked it against the map. "There are times I don't think you could charm the skin off a molting snake. And yet, you usually get enough evidence to convict your suspect. It's amazing."

He flashed her a chilly smile, one calculated to intimidate. "There are other ways of getting information than using charm."

Her brow arched. "Oh? What method did you use on Mr. Hays?

Luke threw the map down onto the seat. "That little weasel? His kind only understands brute force." He put the car in drive and shot out of the parking lot.

"C'mon, Luke, he was unpleasant, but—"

His head whipped around and he pinned her with a stare. "What did you call me?"

Frantically, she searched her mind. What had she called him? *Luke.* How could she have been so stupid? This morning she'd resolved to go back to calling him Detective in an effort to distance herself from him.

"Forget it."

With his right hand he reached over and grasped her arm. "No. You want to know why I didn't like Hays? Lots of funny stuff goes on in that building. Hays sees it, helps it and knows who to call to get those rich, powerful people off the hook when they get in trouble."

She tried to concentrate on his words, but all her brain registered was the feel of his strong, warm fingers manacling her wrist and the pounding of her blood under the pressure of his hand. What would those hands feel like on other, more sensitive, parts of her skin?

That thought brought her imaginings to an abrupt halt. "Let go, McGill."

He glanced at her, then back at the road. "McGill, huh?" His fingers trailed up her arm in a slow caress before he released her.

"We were discussing Mr. Hays and why you think he's breaking the law."

"His attitude. He didn't give a damn I was a cop. The guy was sure of his rights, knew the legal angles and what I could legally do and couldn't. Now, there are three types of people who know that kind of information. Cops and lawyers are two of them, and I think we can rule out those options."

"And the third kind?"

"Jerks who have been arrested countless times. Mr. Hays definitely falls into that category."

As much as she didn't want to admit it, Luke was right. She hadn't liked Mr. Hays and felt there was something not quite kosher about the guy. Score one for the cop.

"All right, I'll concede that Mr. Hays is a questionable character."

Luke snorted.

"But," she continued, ignoring his rude outburst, "while you were locking horns with Mr. Hays, the security guard told me something interesting."

"Oh, what was that?"

She relayed her conversation with the older man.

"That's some good detective work, Counselor."

His praise astounded her. She never would've expected him to acknowledge her skill, let alone compliment it.

Gwen's new apartment was a modest building west of the capitol complex. The woman who let them into the unit had the same bad attitude as Donald Hays.

"I don't know what it is with you police. Can't you just see the place once and get your business done?" She unlocked the apartment door and pushed it open. Her gasp of outrage brought Luke and J.D. rushing into the room.

"Look at this mess!" the woman cried. "It wasn't like this when I let in that other policeman."

The apartment looked much like J.D.'s office had after it had been ransacked.

"Do you remember the officer's name?" Luke asked.

"No. Who remembers that kind of stuff? Well, when Gwen gets back, I'll tell her what happened, but I'm not going to clean this up."

Luke and J.D. looked at each other.

"Mrs. Wilson, Gwen was killed two weeks ago," J.D. quietly said.

The woman put her hands on her hips, obviously outraged. "Why didn't the other policeman tell me? I could've started looking for another renter."

So much for the milk of human kindness, J.D. thought, eyeing the other woman, who was dressed in a housecoat and curlers.

"When we're finished, ma'am, we'll lock up." Luke ushered the woman to the door. "Thank you for your cooperation."

J.D. sighed, discouraged by the mess. "How are we going to find anything in this chaos?"

"We do a systematic search. I'll take this room and the kitchen. You take the bedroom and bathroom. Work from one side of the room to the other. It's simple."

Forty minutes later she didn't think it was as simple as Luke made it out to be. She'd gone through Gwen's dresser, nightstands, closet. All she found out was Gwen had expensive tastes. Her few pieces of jewelry were the real thing—gold and diamonds.

J.D. walked into the living room. Luke was seated at the French provincial desk. She tried not to laugh at the sight of Luke's large frame overpowering the delicate chair. "Did you find anything?"

He glanced up. "Sure did." He tapped the checkbook and bank statement on the desk top. "Gwen Kennedy worked for the liquor lobby. See, here are the check stubs from her paychecks. But if you look at her bank statements, her monthly deposits were nearly twice as large as her paycheck. I can't find any record of the payments, who they were from, but I think that extra money might be the key we need to know what Gwen was involved with."

"She didn't record them in her checkbook?"

"Only the amount. Not who they were from."

"Isn't it on the bank statement?"

"No, just the amount of deposits. No other notations."

J.D. leaned against the desk and picked up a pay stub. "At least the liquor lobby address is here."

"Did you find anything?"

"No, except that Gwen had expensive taste."

"Which she could support. The question is how did she do that?" Luke stood, folded his hands behind his head and stretched. His shirt pulled tight across his chest, outlining his well-defined muscles. J.D.'s awareness of him went up another ten notches.

"Did you search the bathroom?"

"Huh, no." *Witty response, J.D. You sound like a junior high school girl with her first case of puppy love.*

"The sooner we finish here, the sooner we can go question Gwen's employer."

She hurried into the bathroom, frustrated with her sophomoric behavior. Again, Gwen demonstrated her taste for money with her selection of cosmetics. Her brand of makeup couldn't be bought at the local discount store. It was sold only at elegant salons and exclusive department stores.

J.D. pulled out a vanity drawer and glanced at the collection of lip pencils and eye shadows. She was about to close the drawer when she remembered a comment made by a friend who was a private investigator. Check the outside of drawers. She complied, checking the bottom, back and outside of the drawer. Nothing. On impulse, she ran her hand over the inside frame of the cabinet. Bingo. Something round and metal was taped to the wooden frame.

"Ah-ha," she said triumphantly, prying it loose.

"What did you find?" Luke said from the doorway.

Startled, she jerked her hand up, smashing it into the frame. Why on earth was she so nervous?

"I don't appreciate you sneaking up on me, McGill." She thought her voice held the proper amount of censure. He leaned against the wall and gave her a wicked grin.

He didn't utter a word, but his eyes teased her. *So we're back to McGill again?* "What did you find?"

She unclenched her hand and looked at her treasure. "A roll of film."

He took it from her and shook it around in his hand. "A used roll of film."

"That's right. The question is why was it here, taped to the inside of the vanity?"

"She was hiding it from someone."

J.D. had the sinking sensation he was right.

"We need to develop this. Maybe it will give us some answers." He pocketed the roll. "I saw a pharmacy back a street that advertised one-hour film developing. Let's go see what your client was hiding."

J.D. sipped the last of her cola through the much-abused straw. She glanced up at the clock behind the counter. Their pictures would be ready in less than five minutes. Through the window, she could see Luke outside talking on the phone.

"Would you like another cherry cola?" the waitress asked.

"No. But this was delicious. It's been years since I had a real fountain cherry cola."

"Ms. Anderson," the boy behind the counter called, "your pictures are ready."

J.D. paid the youth, took the envelope and joined Luke. He hung up the phone and motioned her toward the car.

With shaking fingers, J.D. pulled out the paste-board sleeve containing the pictures and negatives. Luke rested his arm on the seat back, braced his foot on the floorboard and leaned forward. J.D. felt trapped between his big body and the door. She was aware of every inch of him from the tousled brown hair to the tips of his boots. His well-worn jeans clung to his muscular thighs, allowing her to notice each time he flexed his foot.

His lips curled with a sensual promise that made her head light. And the look in his eyes told her he was aware of the attraction she felt for him and approved. The rat.

He tapped her shoulder. A shiver coursed across her shoulders and down her arms. "You going to look at the pictures or are you going to make me guess what's in them?"

Her body went rigid in an effort to control her blossoming anger. A well-placed elbow would wipe that smug look from his face. "Since I don't think you're that good, I'll show you the pictures."

He threw his head back and laughed. "You're wrong. I'm good."

Ignoring his comment, she opened the yellow folder and pulled out the snapshots. She went through the twenty-four photos slowly. With each shot, she felt the muscles of her stomach tighten with revulsion. When she got to the last one, she let the others fall back into her lap. Her hands went limp at her sides.

The heavy silence in the car pressed in on her chest. What had Gwen been thinking to get involved in this garbage?

Luke rubbed the back of his neck. "What you have there is a pretty damning set of pictures. You know those shots have only one purpose.'' He looked pointedly at her.

She sighed. ''Yes, I know. Blackmail.''

Wi'h his forefinger, Luke tapped the top picture. ''I don't recognize this old fool, but I can guarantee that shapely young lady in bed with him isn't his wife.''

''He's a state senator from somewhere in South Texas. I saw him interviewed last week on TV. He was talking about the bill taxing liquor sales.''

Luke went through the shots of the couple in different positions until he reached the shot of the state senator in a restaurant with three other men. ''Do you recognize any of the other men at the table?''

''No.''

He flipped to the last picture. Only the senator and one man were in the shot. The senator was handing the man a brown envelope. ''This is probably payment for the pictures on the beginning of this roll.''

J.D. gathered up the damning photos and slipped them into their package.

''I'd say your client was into some heavy-duty stuff, Counselor.''

''She admitted she was. But when she came clean, she said she was going to take a lot of people down with her. One of them must have found out what she was going to do and killed her.''

''I think you've got it right. The killer might be one of the men in these pictures.''

J.D.'s head jerked around. ''Why do you say that?''

Luke mentally kicked himself. What was wrong with him to let his tongue run on like that? ''We think that the boot print I was asking Kent Bradley about was left by the killer. A woman wouldn't leave that big or heavy a print.''

"What about the call you made to the Austin police? Were they the ones who searched Gwen's apartment?"

Tapping his fingers against the steering wheel, he shook his head. "Not according to the friend I called. As a matter of fact, Gwen hadn't been reported as missing."

"Probably the same guy who ordered my place searched had Gwen's apartment gone over. Obviously, he's looking for incriminating evidence."

Luke agreed with J.D., but he thought it was probably the killer himself who went through Gwen's things. The ransacking of J.D.'s office had been a hired job. "I asked my friend to send an evidence team over to Gwen's to see if we could lift any usable prints and maybe identify this guy. That means you and I are going to have to be printed so the experts can eliminate ours from the others they find. We can stop by the station on the way to the capitol."

The tall blond man stood and came around his desk, a wide smile on his handsome face. "Luke, it's good to see you. How long has it been? Three, four years?"

Luke shook the man's hand. "It's been five years. I saw you at that workshop in Houston."

"Ah, yes, Houston. My, my, we did have a good time. Who is this gorgeous creature with you? You haven't gotten married, have you?"

Luke choked with horror, his eyes going wide. "Hardly. J.D. Anderson, I'd like you to meet an old friend, Detective Craig Winston."

Craig took J.D.'s hand. "It's a pleasure, ma'am. Luke certainly has improved in his taste in companions."

This was going from bad to worse. Luke wanted to stuff a sock down Craig's throat.

"Down, boy," Luke said. "J.D. is an attorney. A defense attorney who likes to eat cops for breakfast."

Craig studied Luke, then J.D. "I can't believe you have it in for all cops."

Luke waited for J.D. to cut Craig's overblown ego down to size with one of her razor-sharp comments. Instead she gave him a beguiling smile. Was J.D. Anderson flirting? The idea struck Luke as hard as a punch to the gut.

"How perceptive of you, Detective." Her voice was smooth, rich, sexy. Luke gritted his teeth. "Actually, I have nothing against the police. It's illegal search and seizure, coerced confessions and undue force that I object to." Her throaty words sounded like an invitation instead of the censure they were intended to be.

"See, Luke, the lady is reasonable."

He gaped at Craig, who was usually able to pick out a lie at a hundred paces. Why couldn't he see J.D.'s criticism? It was obvious Craig couldn't get past the lady's beauty.

"Depends on which side of the witness stand you see her from," he grumbled, his exasperation starting to show.

Craig slapped Luke on the back. "Lighten up, buddy. Now, why don't you fill me in on the details of the case that brought you two reluctant allies to Austin." Craig grabbed a chair from one of the other desks in the room and set it beside his desk. "Please, sit."

"Thank you, Craig," J.D. said, settling into the chair.

Luke nearly gagged at her saccharine sweetness. What was going on here? Had he missed something?

"Are you going to sit, Luke?" Craig asked.

"Where?" Luke asked, glancing around Craig's desk. There were no other chairs.

Pointing to the next desk, Craig said, "Take Mike's chair."

Luke jerked the chair from under the desk, setting it by J.D.'s. With a few words, he outlined what had happened. "Show him the pictures, J.D. See if he knows any of the people."

She surrendered the package. Craig took his time studying the photos. "Looks like you got yourself a blackmail ring." Finally he was all business.

"That was my conclusion." Luke pinched the bridge of his nose.

"The old guy is Elliot Reynolds. I can't identify the others. Sorry." He held up one shot where the woman's face was clearly captured. "I wouldn't mind meeting her. Of course, it would probably cost me a lot of money."

"You think she's a prostitute?" J.D. asked.

Craig held up his hands. "It's anyone's guess. If you leave one of these pictures here, I'll show it around vice, see if anyone knows her. Anything else?"

"We need you to take our fingerprints for comparison purposes."

"No problem." Craig stood. "Step this way."

A wild thought sprang to life in Luke's brain. Did he dare do it? Oh, yes. He leaned toward Craig. "Do me a favor," he said quietly.

"Sure."

"Let me do the prints on the lady. I've always fantasized about booking her."

One blond brow arched and a knowing smile broke across Craig's face. "That's what I thought, McGill. You've been bit. It's kind of funny, considering who she is."

The comment hit Luke hard, and he drew back. "You're wrong, old friend."

"You think so?"

J.D. wiped the ink from her fingers. "This was a set-up, McGill. I don't believe for a second that Detective Winston had an emergency and that there was no one else in this entire station who could've taken my prints."

He gave her his most innocent look. "What can I say? I just lived out my fondest dream?"

Stepping closer, she whispered in her most seductive voice, "If I lived out my most cherished dream..." She wet her bottom lip.

"Yes?"

"Someone else would be booking me for murder. Yours, Detective. But it might be worth it."

When she tried to move away, he grasped her shoulders. "Counselor, you need better fantasies. And I'll volunteer to help you."

She jerked away. "Forget it, McGill. Now, don't we have some people we need to interview?"

What a pity, he thought as he watched her walk away. Because he was sure he could help improve her fantasies.

Chapter 7

J.D. closed the car door and buckled her seat belt. Imagine Luke trying to teach her about fantasies. He didn't strike her as a man who had much of a creative bent to his life. Opera, plays, the symphony weren't within Luke's realm.

Of course, the fantasies he was talking about were a little earthier, and she didn't doubt that he could show her numerous things she hadn't dreamed.

She turned her head to stare out the side window. What was the matter with her? She didn't want to think of Luke in any way other than as a hostile cop. Unfortunately, she was beginning to have all sorts of crazy thoughts about him. She wondered how it would feel to be wrapped in his strong arms, to have those wonderful whiskey-colored eyes darken with passion just before his lips met hers.

The car door slamming jerked her out of her wanderings. She jumped, and a guilty stain flooded her cheeks. She was grateful that he couldn't read minds.

"Where do you want to go first? Gwen's office or her fiancé's?"

Suddenly she could hear that deep voice whispering tantalizing suggestions into her ear. Whoa, girl!

She glanced at him, and the broad grin on his face made her wonder if he *could* read minds. "It doesn't matter."

"Let's try Hal Weston's office first. Craig said that Weston's office was on the way to the capitol."

"You're the investigator here. I'll trust your judgment."

The look of shock on his face made her want to laugh. "Would you care to repeat that?"

"I don't mind admitting you're the expert here. Part of being good, McGill, is knowing when someone else can do the job better than you."

Approval shone in his eyes. "Sometimes it's hard not to admire you, Counselor."

"But you'll give it your best shot."

He threw his head back and his rich laughter filled the car. "You got it."

Hal Weston's office was in a new high-rise building next to the capitol. Luke gritted his teeth as he took in the upscale decor, from the carpeted hallways to the numbered prints and leather chairs in the lobby. He hated places like this, where the residents thought they could buy anything they wanted. Including justice.

The secretary, a blonde in an expensive suit, greeted them with a well-modulated voice and plastic smile.

"We'd like to see Mr. Weston," Luke informed the woman.

"Do you have an appointment?"

He hated the condescension in her voice. Pulling his badge from his coat pocket, he flashed it in front of Miss High-and-Mighty. "No, but this is police business."

The woman examined the badge. "That is a Dallas shield. Do you have any authority here?"

Luke leaned down. "A woman's been murdered. A woman your boss knew intimately. Now, I could call the local police in here and they can haul your expensive butt in for questioning. Or we can do it the easy way, and you can let me speak to your boss."

The woman's chin shot up. "Well," she huffed before stalking off.

"What's the matter with you, McGill?" J.D. asked. "Is it a personal goal of yours to see how many people you can offend?"

He rubbed the back of his neck. "People like her, who think money can excuse anything, irritate me."

"Is that what you have against me? That my dad has money?"

The corner of his mouth kicked up. "Nope. My feelings for you come from personal experience."

She knew he referred to their skirmishes in court, but the tone of his words evoked feelings that had nothing to do with court battles.

"I'm Perry Odell, Hal's partner." Luke and J.D. turned to the tall man. "May I help you?"

"I'm Detective Lucas McGill of the Dallas Police Department. And this is J.D. Anderson. We need to speak with Mr. Weston about a murder investigation the Dallas police are currently conducting."

"Hal's out of town at the moment. Perhaps I can help?" He motioned to the door at the end of the hall. "Why don't we go into my office and talk."

Luke glanced around the well-appointed room which screamed wealth. He thought of J.D.'s office compared to this one. She came from money, but she didn't flash it like a badge of honor as this man did. He liked that about her.

Luke caught a movement out of the corner of his eye and looked at J.D. She pointed to a photo on the wall. Perry and one of the men in Gwen's pictures were captured holding some sort of plaque alongside the governor.

"Who's the other man in that picture?" Luke asked.

"That's Hal. The governor was giving our firm an award for our fund-raising for local charities." Perry sat on the corner of his desk. "Now, what is this about a murder investigation? Who was murdered?"

"Your partner's ex-live-in girlfriend, Gwen Kennedy." Luke pulled a notebook from his pocket. "Tell me about Mr. Weston's relationship with Ms. Kennedy."

Mr. Odell's fashionably tanned face turned a faint shade of green. "What's to tell? He and Gwen met at some political gathering. They started dating, then about two months later moved in together."

"Do you know why she moved out three weeks ago?" Luke asked.

Picking up a gold-colored pen from his desk, Mr. Odell shook his head. "No. I came back to the office late several weeks ago and heard them arguing, but Hal's door was closed and I didn't hear what the fight was about." He tapped the pen against his leg, and Luke sensed that there was more.

"What else happened, Mr. Odell?"

He lifted his shoulder, trying to appear unconcerned. "The next morning, the building superintendent complained that if there was another occurrence of broken glass and pots in our offices again, he was going to have to charge us an extra cleaning fee."

"So you think the fight between Hal and Gwen escalated into violence where blows were traded?"

"I think they threw things at each other. But that was the only time in the two years they were together that sort of thing happened."

"That you know about," J.D. supplied.

Both men looked at her as if startled by her presence. Mr. Odell nodded.

Luke arched his brow, reminding J.D. who the detective was. She gave him a nod, relinquishing the questioning back to him.

"Thank you," Luke said to J.D. He turned to Perry. "What kind of firm is Weston & Odell?"

"We're a publicity firm that specializes in lobbying. Companies hire us to represent their interests before the legislature. Gwen was also a lobbyist. I think that's why she and Hal hit it off so fast."

Luke stood. "Thank you for your time and help. If I have any more questions, I'll be in touch."

He saw J.D. open her mouth, but before she could say anything, he grasped her elbow and escorted her out of the office.

J.D. tugged her arm from his grip and glared at him. "I don't appreciate being manhandled like that, McGill."

"Sorry." She didn't look very appeased by his apology. "I knew you were going to spill the beans about the pictures, and I don't want Perry Odell to know we have them."

"Why not?"

"Because, Counselor, if he's involved with the blackmail scheme, I didn't want to let him know we have those pictures."

"Then how are we going to find out who the redhead in bed with the senator is?"

The elevator doors slid open. "Trust me. We'll find out."

"Well, that was an exercise in futility," J.D. said. "I've never seen such sidestepping, not since that last time I took guests to the horse barn at the rodeo in Fort Worth. If Gwen's name hadn't been on the door, those people never would've admitted she worked there."

"It's called covering your a—"

"I know what it's called," she snapped, pushing open the lobby door. She plunged into the crowd crossing the street, oblivious to whether Luke followed.

"Where are you going?" he yelled, catching up with her in the middle of the street.

She pointed to the store on the corner. "There."

Luke stopped and stared at the candy store. Why was she going in there? A car horn brought him out of his stupor. He caught sight of J.D.'s shapely backside as she disappeared through the door.

He joined her inside. "What does this have to do with the investigation?"

She rounded on him. "Not a cotton-pickin' thing. I'm frustrated, mad and hungry. And I want some fudge. Got any objections?"

Her expression dared him to say something disparaging. One wrong word and she would rake him up one side and down the other with her razor-sharp tongue. He couldn't blame her for her reaction. He wouldn't mind picking a fistfight with someone just to relieve his own frustration.

He shook his head. "None. As a matter of fact, you can buy me some. With nuts."

The tension drained out of her face and she grinned, reminding him of a naughty child sneaking something past her parents. He felt a corresponding lightness spring to life in him.

After she paid the clerk, she handed him his fudge. Without waiting for him to unwrap his candy, she broke off a large piece of her sinfully dark chocolate treat and popped it into her mouth.

Throwing back her head, she closed her eyes and moaned. "Mmm...heavenly."

The sight of her sensual abandon hit Luke square in the gut. He swallowed, and the sugar and nuts in his mouth went down the wrong way. Instantly, she was by his side, pounding him on the back.

"Are you all right?"

"Yeah."

"You sure?" Concern touched her features.

"Positive."

She shrugged, then broke off another piece of fudge. He watched her reaction again. Although it was not at the level of abandon as her first taste, he could see her give herself over to the pleasure of the treat. Is that how she would look after a thorough loving?

Luke reeled at the thought.

"You're right, Luke."

His eyes flew to her face. She couldn't possibly mean that that's how she'd look after a night of love.

"I'm an addict. But I can't think of anything more pleasant to be addicted to."

"Oh." She was turning his mind to mush, torturing his body by tying it into so many knots it was all but impossible to straighten it out, and putting impossible dreams into his head.

"What do we do next?" J.D. asked.

Luke glanced down Congress Avenue to the capitol building. A special session of the legislature was meeting, giving them a golden opportunity to question the members about Gwen. He pointed to the capitol. "That's our next stop."

"Sounds good to me." She wadded up her sack and tossed it into the trash can. "We might as well walk, because we'll never find a parking space up there."

"Why don't we go up into the gallery and see if we can spot any of the people in Gwen's picture on the senate floor."

Luke was good. He seemed to know how to get to the heart of any matter, even if he did step on toes in his quest. It had become increasingly obvious to her as the day had worn on that Luke didn't tolerate any nonsense from the people he questioned. He was fair and straightforward and expected the same from those he interviewed. "Good suggestion."

His brow arched over those whiskey-colored eyes. His normally cool gaze held a flicker of surprise. She wondered why he was shocked when she acknowledged his expertise. She had never doubted his skill. It was just his methods that she'd challenged in court.

The gallery was empty, with the exception of a couple of spectators and a lone man with a press pass clipped to his sports coat, busily writing on a notepad. He looked up and a wide grin spread across his face. J.D. instantly recognized Steve Banks, a political reporter for one of the major Dallas/Fort Worth television stations.

Steve hooked an elbow over the back of his seat, directing his gaze toward Luke. "What ill wind blew you into town?"

Luke laughed. "We've hit pay dirt, J.D."

"Gold, Luke. That's what I am. Gold."

"Steve, you haven't grown any humbler since you worked the police beat years ago." Luke turned to J.D. "This guy always did have an inflated view of himself. And after he won that award, we exiled him to Austin. Thought his ego would match the ones down here."

The warm camaraderie between the two men made J.D. smile. It wasn't often she'd seen Luke tease someone, let alone allow them to tease him.

Steve pointedly looked over Luke's shoulder at J.D. He rose and extended his hand. "Luke may have no manners, but I do. My name is Steve Banks."

She shook his hand. "I recognized you, Mr. Banks. I'm J.D. Anderson."

Steve rubbed his chin. "You look familiar. You're not in politics, are you?"

"No."

"I should remember a woman as good-looking as you."

J.D. noted the frown on Luke's face the moment before he said, "I heard about your divorce from Ann. I'm sorry."

A bitter chuckle escaped the reporter's lips. "That's what she said—that I was a sorry excuse for a man." He shook off the depressing mood. "What brings you to Austin? You haven't left the Dallas P.D., have you?''

"Nope. J.D. and I are investigating the murder of one of J.D.'s clients. Maybe you can help, since politics is your beat now.''

"Sure. Anything I can do to help.''

"Do you know Gwen Kennedy? She was a lobbyist with the liquor lobby.''

"Yeah, I know her. Gwen is one of the hottest lobbyists here in Austin. She doesn't work strictly for the liquor lobby, though. She also does some independent work. Word is, if you want a bill passed, have Gwen lobby it for you. She has an amazing success record.''

J.D. leaned forward. "So she's thought of highly?''

"Oh, yes.''

"Then why would anyone want to kill her?'' J.D. directed her question at Luke.

Steve went still. "She's dead?''

Luke glared at J.D. before turning back to Steve. "Steve, I'll make a deal with you. I tell you what we know in exchange for your help in identifying some photos we have. But you've got to keep the lid on it for a while. Can you live with that?''

"How long's a while?''

"I've got the feeling this murder isn't going to stand still long. Six weeks at the most.''

With his finger, Steve tapped his lips, considering the deal. "Okay. Tell me what you know.''

Luke quickly filled him in on their sketchy information. When he finished, J.D. handed him the pictures.

"You've got a bomb here, Luke, that's going to blow the roof off this building.''

"Who's the redhead?"

"Gail Williams. She's a lobbyist for the insurance industry. The old fool she's in bed with is Elliot Reynolds. He's the head of the subcommittee that hears bills concerning the insurance industry."

"I'd say there was a slight conflict of interest," J.D. said.

"That's what I'm sure Gail wants," Steve answered.

"You don't sound as if you like her."

Steve's eyes meet J.D.'s. "The lady is a piranha. I always suspected she did more than use pretty words to get her way."

Luke gave J.D. a meaningful look. She glared at him before turning back to Steve. Steve's expression asked what the exchange was all about.

Luke grinned. "J.D.'s been called a piranha a time or two."

J.D. felt the rage building inside her. How dare he! Before she could respond, however, he hastened to add, "Nobody's ever thought you slept with people to get your way. But you have been known to chew people up in court."

"Can we get back to Gail?" J.D. asked, her voice curt. "Where's her office?"

Steve rattled off the address. It was the same building that housed Hal Weston's office.

Luke flipped through the pictures until he got to the men at the restaurant. "Recognize any of them?"

"That's Hal Weston and Elliot Reynolds. But I don't know who the other two men are."

Luke gathered up the pictures and handed them to J.D. to put back into her purse. "I guess our next stop is the office of Senator Reynolds."

"He's not in Austin for the session," Steve informed them. "He had a heart attack last month."

"He's got staff that I can interview."

"Don't count on it, Luke. His daughter—who's older than Gail—is the office manager. Nothing damaging would come out of that office."

"Damn." Luke sighed in exasperation. "I guess that means we have to go interview the lady piranha." He stood. "Let me know if you hear any rumors floating around here that might help."

"You got it."

J.D. said nothing to him as they walked out of the building. The set of her shoulders told him that his comment had offended her. Strangely enough, he was sorry about the crack about the piranha. He grasped her arm and turned her to face him.

"All right. I admit I was out of line in there. You're a darn fine lawyer and I don't like losing cases to you."

"I've never slept with anyone to get my way." He could see her trembling with anger. "I've paid my dues, busting my butt to be twice as good as any man. And do you know what most men's response to my success is? That I used sex to achieve it. Ever even hint it again, McGill, and I'll flatten you so fast, your head will spin."

He didn't respond to the rage vibrating through her. Instead, he keyed in on the hurt. It struck a chord deep inside him. He brushed his finger across her cheek. She froze.

"You're right."

Her eyes fluttered closed. When she opened them, they were brilliant with unshed tears.

"C'mon, lady. We've still got work to do."

She didn't speak, but her watery smile silently thanked him. He swallowed the lump in his throat. The lady could get to him faster than anyone else ever had. It was scary.

Chapter 8

Luke's response effectively burst the bubble of her anger, leaving her disoriented and confused. The compassion and remorse she saw in his eyes pierced through the protective barrier around her heart, touching her deeply. When he caressed her cheek and his soft words fell on her ears, she had wanted to step into his embrace and allow his warmth to take away the bone-deep chill that hovered about her heart.

J.D. recoiled from the thought. From her experience, she knew if a woman surrendered to a man, he'd use that power over her, turning her into a doormat. She'd seen it often enough with her father and his two wives. And, of course, there was her own personal experience with her ex-husband.

"Since Gail's office is only a block over, why don't we walk?"

She stopped and considered Luke's proposal. The rental car was two blocks down Congress Avenue. It was just as easy to walk to Gail's office as to hike to the car and drive back. She pulled off her high heels. "I'm ready when you are."

"You'll ruin your stockings that way."

She started walking toward the office building. "Oh? What do you know about women's panty hose?"

He waggled his eyebrows. "More than you think I should."

"Well, I'd rather ruin my hose than my feet."

He shook his head. "You continue to amaze me."

"Why?"

"Because most of the really smart people I know don't have a lick of sense. You seem to have both."

With each word he uttered, he was burrowing deeper into her heart, and she had no idea how to stop him.

They were crossing the parking lot of Gail's building when Luke reached out and stopped her. She sensed his urgency. "Look," he said, pointing to the couple standing by a black limousine. J.D. got a good look at the woman's face as she slid into the back seat.

"That's Gail Williams."

"And the gentleman getting into the limo with her isn't Elliot Reynolds," Luke added.

"Do you know him?"

Luke shook his head. "No."

"Rats." She set her shoes on the asphalt and slipped them on.

"What are you doing?"

"I'm going up to Ms. Williams's office to see if I can pump the secretary for any information. I thought I'd be less suspicious if I had shoes on. Got any objections?"

"Give it your best shot, Counselor."

She started toward the main entrance and noticed that he hadn't followed. "Come on, McGill."

"I thought I'd stay here."

She strode back to his side and clasped his arm. "You're coming with me, Detective. I'm going to need you."

A frown wrinkled his brow. "For what?"

A mysterious smile curved her mouth. "Wait and see."

From his somber expression, it was obvious he wasn't eager to discover what she had in store.

Gail's office was two floors above Hal Weston's. Through the clear glass doors, J.D. could see three secretaries at their desks with five offices branching off the main room.

Studying the women, J.D. asked, "Which one do you think is Gwen's secretary?"

"This is your show, J.D. Take a guess."

She threw him a disgruntled look. "Thanks." Taking a deep breath, she pushed open the door. "Go along with me, no matter what," she whispered, wrapping her arm around his.

J.D. didn't like the gleam that appeared in his eyes, nor the upward turn at the corner of his mouth.

"May I help you?" the first secretary, a young, pretty brunette, asked.

J.D. put on her I'm-going-to-charm-the-pants-off-you face. "Yes. I was wondering if Gail Williams was in? I don't have an appointment, but Gail and I went to high school together. I'm only in Austin for a few hours and wanted her to meet my charming fiancé."

"I'm sorry, Ms.—"

"Campbell. Rita Campbell."

Luke's head jerked around and, without looking at him, she slid her hand up the inside of his arm and pinched him. His elbow flew out, knocking J.D. sideways.

Luke caught her before she stumbled into the desk. "Are you all right, sweetheart?" he asked in an annoyingly pleasant voice.

Reaching deep within, J.D. composed herself. "Yes." The word sounded normal. She threw the secretary an apologetic smile. "I'm not used to high heels."

The woman laughed. "I know the feeling, Ms. Campbell. As I was saying, Ms. Williams just left for the day. She won't be back in the office until Wednesday."

"Oh dear, and I so wanted to see her." Luke better not roll his eyes, she thought, hearing her own inane words. She turned to him. "I guess you won't be able to meet Gail, sweetheart. We'll just have to fly back to L.A."

"Ms. Campbell, is your flight leaving anytime soon?"

"Around two," Luke supplied.

"Then perhaps you'll see her at the airport. Maybe you'll even be on the same flight. I think Ms. Williams's flight to Las Vegas continues on to L.A."

"Oh, what airline?"

The secretary named the airline.

"That's wonderful. That's the same one we're taking. Thank you for your help. I'll be sure to tell Gail what a wonderful help you were."

J.D. was beaming as they rode the elevator down to the ground floor.

"I didn't know you had it in you, J.D. You should've been an actress, if that performance was any indication of your skills."

She laughed. "Are you trying to say I'm a terrific liar?"

"You could've fooled me, especially when you called me sweetheart." His voice was low and intimate.

Pointing her finger at him, she warned, "Don't get any ideas, McGill." And yet, the word *sweetheart* rolling off her tongue had felt right. As a matter of fact, the entire scenario had felt right.

J.D. kicked off her shoes. "Turn around."

"Why?"

"Because I'm going to take off my panty hose."

Reluctantly, he turned toward the elevator doors, leaving her at the back.

"Do you have any particular reason for your actions?"

"It will make running back to the car easier."

The elevator stopped at the second floor and a man tried to get on. J.D. squeaked and moved to the front corner of the elevator. Luke blocked the man's path. "Sorry, but you'll have to catch the next one down."

J.D. leaned her head back against the control panel. "Thanks, Luke."

He glanced at her. Her skirt was halfway up her thighs and her panty hose were bunched around her knees. She made quite a picture. "You're welcome. Only next time, could you wait until you're someplace more private to undress?"

She chuckled and finished taking off her hose.

"Now, why do we have to run to the car?" Luke asked, trying to ignore her movements.

The elevator doors opened. J.D. stuffed her panty hose into her purse, gathered up her shoes and ran into the lobby. "I plan to be on that flight to Las Vegas."

"That's crazy," he yelled at her back.

He didn't get a chance to further discuss it with her because she sprinted across the parking lot and down the street. For a little bitty thing, she sure could run. He felt like a fool running after her—an exquisitely dressed woman with bare legs, who ran like a demon. But what could he do? Yell at her to stop? Tackle her on the cement sidewalk?

He was breathing hard when he reached the car. "Someone ought to spank your butt," he said between shuddering gasps.

"Quit with the sermon and unlock the doors."

He glared at her over the roof of the car as he inserted the key into the lock. When she slid into the seat next to him, he noticed she was only slightly winded, whereas he couldn't draw enough oxygen into his lungs. Once he could see straight, he started the car.

"Now, what is this crazy idea that you have?" he asked, pulling into traffic.

"This lead is too good to let drop. Gail was obviously going off for some sort of liaison with that man. And I'm sure if we got that guy's picture and showed it to Steve, he'd tell us Gail's latest love interest was a member of the legislature."

"You don't know that for sure."

"Give me a break, McGill. I bet that sixth sense of yours is screaming at you right now that we've stumbled onto something important here."

Checking his rearview mirror, Luke floored the gas pedal as he merged with the traffic on the highway. As much as he hated to admit it, J.D. was right. "This isn't some TV cop show, lady, where I can go zipping off to Las Vegas on a whim. I'd have to clear it with my superiors."

"And by the time the okay would come back, Gail and her friend will be back in Austin. Well, you may have those constraints, McGill, but I don't."

"Ah, hell, J.D. You go to Las Vegas and my sixth sense tells me you're going to get into some major-league trouble."

That set her off. "As I've told you before, I can take care of myself." Her words were like blocks of ice, chilling and hard.

He ought to say the hell with her, let her board the plane to Dallas and let her fend for herself. He considered it as he drove to the airport and parked the car. As he watched her stride into the terminal building, he knew he couldn't abandon her to the trouble that was brewing.

He muttered a crude word, then followed her. Inside, J.D. wasn't hard to spot. She was the only person at the ticket counter.

"Is there any room left on your two-thirty flight to Las Vegas?"

The man behind the counter typed the information into his keyboard. "Yes, madam, there's an available seat."

"Are there two?" Luke asked.

The man's head came up. "I'm sorry, sir, I didn't see you standing there. Yes, there are several open seats on the plane. Would you like to purchase two tickets?"

"Yes," J.D. answered, slapping down her bank credit card.

Luke placed his hand over the plastic card. "I can pay."

"I don't doubt that you can, McGill. But I do doubt you have that much cash on you, knowing cops as I do. Let me buy the tickets and you can pay me back later, with interest if that will help soothe your masculine ego. But right now we have to get on that flight."

He wanted to argue with her, but, unfortunately, he didn't own a bank credit card because he didn't believe in them. He had the cash in a savings account, but that would have to wait until they got back to Dallas.

"You win, J.D. But I'll pay interest." He handed her card to the clerk.

"I didn't doubt it for a minute," she mumbled.

"Do you have luggage?" the airline clerk asked.

. Luke glared at him. "No, this is a spur-of-the-moment thing." As if the idiot couldn't tell. "I'm taking the lady to Las Vegas to get married. Couldn't you guess from our loving attitude?"

The man flinched at the tone of Luke's voice.

J.D. drove her elbow into his ribs. "Behave yourself, McGill," she said, accepting their tickets from the clerk.

They were held up several minutes at the metal detectors while Luke showed the guard his service revolver and badge. After he was okayed, they moved quickly to the gate, where the flight was in the process of boarding.

J.D. craned her neck but couldn't see over the crowd of people. "Do you see them?"

He shook his head.

"They'd better be on this flight."

Luke echoed her sentiment.

They saw nothing of their quarry until they boarded the plane and walked through first class. On the next to the last row of that section sat Gail Williams with her latest "escort."

Luke didn't know whether to be relieved or depressed. They were on the right plane, but for the next two hours he was going to suffer the same torture that had nearly driven him wild this morning. J.D. would be inches from him, filling his senses, making his body want things that were just flat impossible.

It was going to be a long afternoon.

J.D. plowed through the throng of people at McCarrin International Airport, panic clawing at her heart. "Where did they go?" The sound of slot machines punctuated her words.

"They probably had luggage. Let's try the baggage claim area."

Immediately she located the sign, pointing out where they needed to go. It was comforting to have Luke here with her. Throughout the day, he was always sure of his direction. He may not have handled all the people with kid gloves, but his instincts hadn't been wrong.

"Do you see them?" she asked, frustrated that she couldn't see over the sea of bodies. Luke didn't have that problem. He easily saw over most people's heads.

"Yeah, there they are, going out the door."

J.D. raced to the glass wall and watched the couple climb into a cab. She memorized the company name and the number of the vehicle. Grabbing his hand, she pulled him outside and flagged down another cab.

Two taxis pulled up to the curb. J.D. made a beeline to the second one.

Luke shrugged his shoulders as if apologizing to the first cabbie and followed her.

"Where do you want to go?" the driver asked.

"Well, I have a bit of a problem. You see, we are going to surprise some friends and help them celebrate their anniversary. Gail's husband arranged the surprise, but in typical male style, he forgot to tell us what hotel they were staying at. But I did see them leave the airport in one of your taxis. Number twenty-seven. Could you call your dispatcher and see where they went?"

The man rolled his eyes, then shook his head.

"There's an extra twenty dollars if you take us to the same hotel," Luke said, his voice sure and confident.

The man glanced at Luke, and an understanding look passed between the two men. The driver called and got the name of the hotel.

Once on the road, J.D. moved closer to Luke. His arm rested along the top of the seat.

"He didn't believe me, did he?" she asked, leaning nearer. She had only meant to get close enough to prevent the driver from overhearing her. Instead, J.D. found herself plunged into a heated world of sensation. His body heat surrounded her, making her blood flow faster. His scent, strong and masculine, filled her nostrils, bringing to mind the picture of him standing on the ladder, his bare chest sparkling in the sunlight. Her eyes focused on his mouth. She relived the kiss they shared, and her muscles seemed to melt.

His arm came down, resting on her shoulders. His mouth moved to her ear. "No, he didn't."

For a moment she had no idea what he was talking about. Her eyes met his. "What?" A frown settled between her brows.

"The driver didn't believe the story you made up."

"So you bribed him."

His other hand came up, and with a gentle touch, he stroked the line of her chin. "I spoke the language he knew."

Everything in her body went still except for the nerve endings in the small stretch of skin he touched. Her breathing stopped, her mind ceased functioning and her heart suspended its beating.

"Oh, no," the driver said, bringing the real world into focus again.

She bounded away from Luke, as if she'd been shot from a cannon, and slid across the seat.

"What's wrong?" Luke asked.

The cabbie pulled the car to the shoulder of the road. "The engine overheated. I'll call another unit to come pick you up and take you to your hotel." He winked at Luke.

J.D. threw open the door and climbed out. She kept her back to the men, afraid the guilty flush in her cheeks would give away her humiliation to Luke and the driver. What had come over her to act like such a gushing ninny? As she stared out into the desert, she prayed that a hole would open up and swallow her.

J.D. glanced at her watch. Twenty minutes had passed since they called for a backup cab. She felt a rising sense of panic envelop her. Gail and her victim were going to get away.

She faced the driver. "What's taking so long?"

"He'll be here any minute."

"You said that ten minutes ago."

The man shrugged. "Traffic must be bad."

She whirled to stare out at the endless horizon.
Hugging her waist, she felt her sheer blouse stick to
her skin. She glanced down at her five-hundred-dollar
suit. The side seam was torn, presumably from her
mad dash to the car in Austin. The navy blue material
was dirty and rumpled. Her eyes went to her bare legs.
What a sight she must be.

Strong hands settled on her shoulders, turning her.
She looked up at Luke. He studied her, his eyes traveling over her face and down her body. His fingers dug
into the tight muscles of her neck.

"Relax, Counselor." His eyes were tender and his
mouth curved into a reassuring smile. "Your worry-
ing yourself sick isn't going to change a thing. It won't
make that cab get here any quicker. Even if it did, you
wouldn't be any use to me sick. I promise, we're not
going to lose them."

She gave herself over to his clever fingers and comforting words.

His hands moved up her neck, causing several hair-
pins to fall to the asphalt. Quickly, he picked the other
pins from her hair and ran his fingers down the length
of it.

Her heart stopped.

"You look hot. Why don't you take off your
jacket."

Before she could protest, he'd unbuttoned the coat
and slipped it from her shoulders. Under the sheer
pink shirt with pearl buttons, the lace of her camisole
could be seen clearly.

She glanced down. It wasn't too bad, she thought,
until she looked back at Luke. His amber-colored eyes
had turned almost black with heat—a heat she could

feel in every fiber of her being. The air around them was charged with clashing emotions.

A horn blast drew their attention.

"Your cab is here."

J.D. clutched her jacket to her chest and walked to the late-model car. Luke followed.

They said nothing to each other as the driver started the car and shot into traffic. J.D. squirmed in the seat, trying to free her hair from under her hips. Her mind was reeling from what had happened between her and Luke back on the roadside.

Knowing she must look like a wanton hussy, she opened her purse and rummaged through it until she found a large silver hair clasp. Setting it on her lap, she gathered her hair and twisted it into a tight rope. With a flick of her wrist, she wound the thick rope into an *S* at the back of her head, securing it with the clasp.

As she worked, she felt Luke's gaze on her and knew he regretted her putting up her hair.

Once her hair was secured, J.D. breathed a sigh of relief. She was in control again and not barreling headlong into an area of sexual intrigue she knew absolutely nothing about.

Out of the corner of her eye, she could see Luke resting against the door. He looked calm, even relaxed, and she was dying to know what was going on inside his head.

Why was it that with a single touch, a look, Luke McGill could make her feel things that no other man had? Did her presence have the same effect on him that his had on her?

Don't be stupid, J.D.

Whether or not she had an effect on him, her head told her to keep her distance from the man. If she didn't, and lost control of the situation, of the relationship, then she would become just another victim, much like her mother. And that, J.D. reassured herself, was a fate that would never befall her.

The cab pulled under the covered driveway, stopping in front of the hotel's main entrance. After paying the driver, Luke and J.D. walked into the massive lobby.

"A little overdone." The words slipped out of J.D.'s mouth as she took in the surroundings.

One corner of Luke's mouth kicked up. "A little." The place looked like something out of a thirties' movie set.

"What now?" she asked. "Where do we begin?"

"Let's see if Ms. Williams registered under her own name. That will tell us whether the lady wants anonymity or not."

It was a long shot, Luke knew. The clerk behind the front desk would balk at letting them know the suspect's room number, and he didn't want to flash his badge and have hotel security hot on his heels.

Luke gave the girl his most charming smile. "We were to meet some friends here and spend the week. I was wondering if they've checked in."

"Their name, sir."

"Gail Williams and party."

The girl typed in the name. "I'm sorry, but no Ms. Williams is registered, nor do I see any reservations in her name for this week."

"Maybe I got the name of the hotel wrong. Thanks." He took J.D.'s arm and led her away. "That tells us our lady friend is up to no good."

"Too bad we don't know the man's name."

Luke shook his head. "You can count on one thing, Counselor. If Gail doesn't want her name recorded in the hotel records, her companion won't, either." He glanced around the room. "We can check the casino and bars, and if they're not there, then we'll camp out in the lobby until they show up." She did not look convinced. "Don't worry, we'll find them."

"I wish I shared your confidence."

He wished he did, too.

They found their quarry in the third bar they tried. Luke pulled J.D. down into a booth where they had an unobstructed view of the other couple. A waiter materialized and took their order—a coffee and a cola.

"I wish I could hear what they're saying."

"You'll have to settle for tailing them, J.D. I doubt if we could talk either one into wearing a wire so we could have evidence to convict them."

She wrinkled her nose at him. "You're *so-o-o* funny."

Resting his forearms on the table, he leaned forward. "I try."

Their drinks were delivered, stopping the conversation.

"How are we going to—" She swallowed the rest of the sentence.

Luke stiffened when he saw a tall, blond man in an expensive suit walk up to Gail's table.

"Oh, no," J.D. groaned.

Luke threw her a puzzled look.

"Keep watching," she whispered in a strained voice. "I need to leave."

She started to rise when the blond man's head jerked up, and he pinned her with his eyes. J.D. moaned and settled back in her chair.

Luke wanted to ask her what was wrong, but before he could get the words out, the mystery man was at their table.

"This is a surprise."

The words rang false.

"I can't believe you're here in Las Vegas," the blond said coolly, his perfect smile showing pearly whites. "Is there a lawyers' convention? I don't recall one."

"No, I'm not here for a convention," J.D. answered, her words stilted.

"Well, you can't possibly be here to gamble, since I know how much you hate gambling." The man's nasty tone grated on Luke's nerves. His instinctive reaction would have been to jump up and punch the jerk in the mouth, but that sixth sense of his warned him against any rash actions. Besides, he knew J.D. wouldn't appreciate his interference.

"What I hated and objected to," she countered in a steely voice, "was gambling away our rent money three months in a row."

"There wouldn't have been a problem if you weren't too damn proud to ask your rich daddy for more."

J.D.'s eyes turned icy blue, cold enough to freeze everyone within a hundred feet. She stood, her back straight, her chin up. "That's all you ever wanted, wasn't it, Allen? My father's money. Tell me, why are you here—since you're the one who had the gambling problem, not me?"

The situation was deteriorating at an alarming rate. Luke knew that if he didn't act fast, J.D. would blow their chance to discover why Gail was in Vegas. Standing, Luke held out his hand. "I'm Lucas McGill. And you're . . . ?"

"Allen Danford." He ignored Luke's hand, turning back to J.D. "Why are you here, J.D.? What possible reason could you have for being here?"

Luke had an uneasy feeling. Allen Danford had an unhealthy interest in why J.D. was in Vegas.

"I am not accountable to you."

Out of the corner of his eye, Luke caught the movement of the couple they'd been observing. They stood and started toward their table.

"You can't possibly be here for a lovers' tryst, since I know how frigid you are."

He would pay back Allen Danford for that insult, Luke vowed, but now was not the time.

J.D.'s eyes went black with rage. *Be calm, Counselor,* he silently urged her. *Don't blow this opportunity.*

"Allen, is there a problem?" Gail queried as she stepped to his side.

"I don't know," he answered. A look passed between Gail and Allen that set Luke's teeth on edge. "I was just trying to find that out."

Gail studied J.D. "Do you know these people, Allen?"

He nodded. "Gail Williams, Bill Frank, may I present my ex-wife, J.D. Anderson."

J.D. shook their hands, then introduced Luke.

Frowning, Gail asked, "Didn't I see you two in Austin this morning?"

They were in hot water now. If Luke didn't miss his guess, Allen was somehow tied in with Gail Williams. And they both were suspicious of him and J.D.

Only one plausible answer for their being in Vegas
came to mind. He didn't know if J.D. would go along
with it, but it was worth a try. "No, we were in Dallas
this morning. That is—" Luke grabbed J.D.'s hand
and laced his fingers through hers "—until I asked
J.D. to marry me."

J.D. gaped at him. Afraid her stunned expression
would give them away, Luke lean over and kissed her
behind her ear. "Play along," he whispered. Then he
added more loudly, "I know you wanted to keep this
a secret, sweetheart, but I'm afraid the cat's out of the
bag."

He released her hand, then slipped his arm around
her waist, drawing her close. Glancing around the
gathered group, he said, "When she accepted, we
hopped the first plane to Vegas."

Allen Danford looked like someone had kicked him
in the seat of his perfectly pressed slacks, and Luke
took a great deal of pleasure in his reaction.

Bill pumped both Luke's and J.D.'s hands. "Con-
gratulations."

"I don't see a ring on J.D.'s finger," Allen pointed
out, his voice carrying a sour note.

"We've yet to do the deed," Luke explained, wagging his brows. "We thought we'd catch our breath
before trying to find a chapel."

"That's wonderful," Bill said. "Isn't this great?"
he asked Gail and Allen. "I haven't been to a wedding in ages." He rubbed his hands together.

"Gail, isn't there a chapel just past the hotel?" Allen asked.

"Yes, I believe there is one."

"Oh, you don't need to go to any trouble," Luke
told the trio.

Bill went still. "Forgive me. I didn't mean to strong-arm your wedding."

"Oh, but I think their eloping is so romantic." Gail's words were tinged with venom. "I'd love to see you two get married—that is, if you don't have any objections."

"We'd be honored to be your witnesses," Bill offered.

Luke glanced at J.D., expecting her to come up with some valid excuse that would get them off the hook. Instead, J.D. wound her arms around Luke's waist. As she smiled shyly at the three witnesses, her fingers, which were beneath Luke's jacket, dug into his waist. He tried not to flinch. He felt fortunate that she didn't snatch his gun from the holster and shoot him with it.

"That's very nice of you, Mr. Frank. Luke and I appreciate your thoughtfulness."

Luke couldn't believe his ears. She was agreeing to let these people cart them off to some chapel and be witnesses to their marriage. Maybe he'd heard wrong.

When his eyes met hers, he read her message clearly. *You got us into this mess. You can darn well get us out.*

Terrific. The one time he needed the contrary female to come up with a brilliant idea, and she'd tossed the ball into his court.

Too bad, because he didn't have the slightest idea how to get them out of this mess.

Chapter 9

Was she out of her mind to let Allen railroad her into marrying Luke? J.D. wondered as she stared out the window of the limousine. Well, if she was honest with herself, Allen hadn't been the culprit. Luke had put his foot in his mouth all by himself. After Bill Frank jumped on the bandwagon, there'd been no turning back without jeopardizing the whole murder investigation.

But why couldn't she have come up with some valid reason for the three musketeers not to accompany her and Luke to the chapel? She was a bright, golden-tongued lawyer. She should've come up with something.

That is, if you'd really wanted to, a little voice in her head taunted.

That's ridiculous, she argued back, but she couldn't deny the thrill that ran up her spine when Luke had announced they were in Las Vegas to be married.

What she really wanted to do was tell the driver to stop the car and let her out, but Allen's smug expression kept her silent.

Somehow, someway, her ex-husband was involved with Gail Williams. And he'd probably known Gwen.

"What are you doing with yourself these days, Allen? Did you find another rich wife to help you finish law school?"

Bill's and Gail's shocked eyes flew to J.D. She felt Luke nudge her, reminding her not to blow it at this late date. But she didn't care. They needed to know what Allen did for a living and if he was somehow connected with Gwen.

Allen's smile looked as artificial as Gail's fingernails. "I'm an administrative assistant to Senator Sam W. Thomas. And no, I haven't married again. Once was more than enough." The words were knife-sharp, slicing through her heart. "And yes, I finished law school."

She wondered how many exams he'd bought.

J.D.'s heart sank when she saw the ironically named True Love Chapel. From the grin on Allen's face, he was enjoying every moment of her humiliation. The tiny wood structure, painted hot pink, with hearts decorating the doors, bore little resemblance to the stately old church with soaring stained-glass windows in Midland, where she and Allen had exchanged vows.

Luke leaned around J.D. and gazed at the building. His brow arched and he turned his head, meeting J.D.'s eyes.

"A bit garish, don't you think? Not the kind of place we wanted to get married in, is it, J.D.?"

"It definitely isn't what I envisioned."

"Why don't we try to find a place a little less...uh...showy."

She had an overwhelming urge to kiss Luke.

He tapped the driver on the shoulder. "Do you think you can find another chapel with a bit more dignity?"

The man nodded and found a small non-denominational chapel less than a mile away.

There, the minister welcomed the group. Then before J.D. and Luke could protest, his wife began playing the organ.

J.D. kept waiting for Luke to come up with some valid reason why they couldn't get married or why the three musketeers couldn't be present. Only when the ceremony began and she listened to him say his vows did she realize he wasn't going to come up with any excuse.

Luke's strong voice resonated throughout the room, warming her. As she heard herself repeat the words promising to love and honor, she wished for a fleeting instant the vows she spoke were true.

"Do you have rings?" the minister asked.

"No," Luke answered. "We were in too much of a hurry to think about the incidentals."

"That's all right. By the power vested in me, I now pronounce you man and wife. You may now kiss your bride."

The words broke through her stupor. She looked up into Luke's eyes. Something she couldn't quite identify flashed in their depths. His large, strong hands cupped her face. Slowly his head descended and his lips covered hers.

The room and the people in it ceased to exist for J.D. Her world consisted only of her and Luke. His

NO RISK, NO OBLIGATION TO BUY ... NOW OR EVER!

CASINO JUBILEE
"Scratch'n Match" Game

Here's how to play:

1. Peel off label from front cover. Place it in space provided at right. With a coin, carefully scratch off the silver box. This makes you eligible to receive two or more free books, and possibly another gift, depending upon what is revealed beneath the scratch-off area.

2. Send back this card and you'll receive brand-new Silhouette Intimate Moments® novels. These books have a cover price of $3.50 each, but they are yours to keep absolutely free.

3. There's no catch. You're under no obligation to buy anything. We charge nothing – ZERO – for your first shipment. And you don't have to make any minimum number of purchases – not even one!

4. The fact is, thousands of readers enjoy receiving books by mail from the Silhouette Reader Service™ months before they're available in stores. They like the convenience of home delivery and they love our discount prices!

5. We hope that after receiving your free books you'll want to remain a subscriber. But the choice is yours – to continue or cancel, anytime at all! So why not take us up on our invitation, with no risk of any kind. You'll be glad you did!

YOURS FREE!

This lovely Victorian pewter-finish miniature is perfect for displaying a treasured photograph – and it's yours absolutely free – when you accept our no-risk offer.

CASINO JUBILEE
"Scratch'n Match" Game

CHECK CLAIM CHART BELOW FOR YOUR FREE GIFTS!

YES! I have placed my label from the front cover in the space provided above and scratched off the silver box. Please send me all the gifts for which I qualify. I understand that I am under no obligation to purchase any books, as explained on the back and on the opposite page.

245 CIS AKYR (U-SIL-IM-08/93)

Name _____

Address _____ Apt. _____

City _____ State _____ Zip _____

▼ DETACH AND MAIL CARD TODAY! ▼

mouth was gentle and coaxing. But before she could respond, he pulled away. His gaze held hers for a moment before he turned to the others.

Grinning broadly, Bill patted Luke on the back. "It's so good to see young people in love."

Luke simply nodded.

"Well, c'mon, folks. Let me treat everyone to a drink. We'll toast the new bride and groom."

In the silence of the limo on their way back to the hotel, J.D.'s stomach growled. Every head turned to look at her. Luke watched in amazement as J.D.'s face turned scarlet. His heart went out to her. She had put up with a lot of garbage this afternoon, her ex-husband topping the list.

He put his arm around her shoulders. "With the exception of a piece of fudge, J.D. and I haven't eaten all day." The way he worded it, it sounded like he'd spent the night with her. From the narrowing of Allen's eyes, her ex thought as much.

Too bad.

"So, J.D. still has a thing for chocolate, huh?" Allen asked.

It's none of your damn business, Luke wanted to growl in the man's face. "C'mon, Danford. You don't expect husband number two to discuss his wife's little quirks with husband number one. Why, it just isn't gentlemanly, is it Bill?"

Bill laughed. "He's got you there, Allen. Well, if you two haven't eaten today, let me treat you to dinner."

It was a good opening for Luke and J.D. to discover how these three were connected. "That's very generous of you, Bill. What do you say, sweetheart? Want to eat?''

J.D. looked thunderstruck. "You're asking me?"

"Why wouldn't I?" Why was she making a big deal over his asking what she wanted to do?

Her lips curved into a smile that made his toes curl and his blood go hot. "I'd like that."

During the balance of the ride, Luke's gaze alternated between J.D. and Allen. He found Allen's intimate knowledge of her distasteful and disturbing. It seemed a desecration of her life that someone like Allen Danford would know her deepest thoughts and actions.

But what really touched a raw spot in Luke was that Allen's knowledge of J.D.'s addiction to chocolate seemed to intrude on his relationship with her—whatever that relationship was.

No matter how hard he tried to envision it, Luke couldn't see J.D. with Danford—the most obnoxious, self-centered, self-absorbed man he'd ever run across, and that was going some. What had J.D. ever seen in him, aside from his godlike good looks? Once you got past the physical perfection of the man, there was nothing to admire on the inside.

And he certainly couldn't imagine J.D. taking any trash off this guy. Yet, from their conversation, he knew she had. Why?

Love, a little voice in his head answered. People do strange things when they think they are in love. Had that happened to J.D.? Or had she put up with Allen because she didn't want to admit she'd failed like her father had implied?

The questions nagged at him the rest of the way back to the hotel. When Bill suggested they eat in the hotel restaurant, no one objected. The conversation over dinner was bland and inconsequential until Gail asked, "What do you do for a living, Luke?"

Luke glanced up from his steak. Gail's expression was one of polite interest, but he had this itch between his shoulders that told him the lady had ulterior motives.

Before he could think of a creative lie, J.D. said, "Luke works with me."

A spark of irritation flashed in Gail's eyes. "And what do you do, J.D.?"

Gail's reaction perked J.D. up. "Why, I'm a defense attorney. Luke helps me with my cases, don't you, dear?"

Ah, she was good. With anyone else, telling the truth would've given them away. J.D. simply stated the facts, putting her particular slant on it, and voilà— truth took on a whole new meaning.

He couldn't hide his pleasure at her response. "Indeed I do. I try my hardest to give you ammunition to use in court."

J.D. choked on her potato. Her watery eyes fixed on his face, then she burst into laughter.

"I didn't know I asked so humorous a question," Gail complained.

"You didn't," Luke said. "It's just that J.D. and I like to tease each other about our work. Speaking of work, what do you do, Gail?"

She carefully set her fork on her plate. "I'm a lobbyist for the insurance industry."

"In Texas?" Luke asked.

Her smile strained, she answered, "Yes."

"Ah, yes. You mentioned Austin earlier. How careless of me not to have made the connection."

Gail's expression was as stiff as the hundred-proof hooch brewed in the backyards of some East Texas homes. "If you will excuse me for a moment, I need to powder my nose."

"That sounds like a good idea," J.D. said. She placed her napkin on the table. "I'll go with you."

Gail's lips compressed into a tight line, yet she voiced no objection. Once in the ladies' restroom, J.D. took down her hair and ran a brush through it.

"I take it you met Allen in Austin at some political function," J.D. casually threw out, working the tangles from her hair.

Gail paused in applying her lipstick. "Not really. Since I'm a lobbyist, I regularly go to each senator's office. With Allen the administrative assistant for Senator Thomas, our paths often cross."

J.D. tried to sound casual as she asked, "Well, what are you, Allen and Bill doing here in Las Vegas?"

Gail whirled to face J.D. "If you must know, Bill and I came to be together. The reason we didn't broadcast it was because Bill's wife would use it against him in their divorce. As to why Allen is here, I don't have a clue. Since he knows both Bill and me, he came over to say hello. That's when he saw you and we started this marathon."

J.D. wanted to hold Gail's red head under the cold-water tap for a few minutes. It might improve her attitude. "I can assure you, Ms. Williams, the idea of having my ex-husband at my wedding to Luke was the last thing I wanted."

"Good. Then we can part company soon." Gail pulled open the door, and J.D. was seized with the urge to place her foot in the middle of Ms. Williams's backside. Fortunately for Gail, a very pregnant woman appeared at the door beside her, and J.D. decided not to risk hurting the innocent.

The table was empty when she and Gail returned. Immediately the waiter appeared. "The gentlemen," he explained, "went next door to the lounge. They asked for you ladies to join them. Mr. McGill told me to tell you, ma'am, that he has your chocolate cheesecake with him."

J.D.'s brow arched. "A bribe?"

The waiter nodded. "I think that's what he said."

A chuckle escaped J.D.'s lips. Luke knew her a little too well.

The room was dim, filled with smoke, murmured conversations and couples locked in embraces, swaying on the dance floor to the romantic ballad being played.

The men were sitting in a booth next to the dance floor. Luke stood and waved them over to the table.

"You gave me a shock moving like that," J.D. told them.

"Afraid husband number two already had deserted you?" Allen asked.

A deadly silence greeted Allen's question.

"If you want to keep that nose of yours pretty, apologize, Danford." The deadly tone of Luke's voice left no doubt that he meant every word.

"Allen," Bill said. "I'm surprised at you. I've never heard you be so rude to anyone."

That's because he's already squeezed this sucker dry, J.D. thought.

"You're right, Bill," Allen graciously responded. "I don't know what came over me. I'm sorry, J.D."

Baloney, you don't know what came over you, J.D. wanted to shout back. Instead, she nodded her acceptance because she knew her voice would betray her skepticism.

"Would you like to dance, sweetheart?" Luke asked.

She wanted to kiss him right there for his timely intervention. "I'd love to."

Luke led her onto the dance floor. Wrapping his arm around her waist, Luke pulled J.D. close.

"What are you doing?" she said through clenched teeth.

Luke grabbed her free hand and tucked it close to his chest. "Hush," he softly commanded. "We have an audience and we better make this good."

He was right. With a heavy sigh, she slipped her free hand under his arm to rest on the broad muscles of his back.

"What happened in the restroom that put such a mean look on Gail's face?"

From the tone of his voice, it was obvious that Luke thought she'd done something intentional to offend Gail. "I simply asked her how she met Allen."

His fingers tipped up her chin. "What was her answer?"

"Through work."

His knowing eyes searched hers. She wanted to squirm under the intensity, but resolutely refused to crumble.

"What else happened, J.D., that you're not telling me?"

"I asked why she was in Vegas."

Luke's chin dropped to his chest and he moaned.

"It's not that bad," she said in defense of her actions. He was acting like she'd blown the whole thing.

Heaven knew not much else could go wrong in this episode.

"Why didn't you just tell her we were following her to see what illegal activity she was going to commit today?"

"Do you want to hear what she said or not? Or would you rather trade barbs?"

"Tell me."

"She said that we were interfering with her affair with the senator and to buzz off."

Luke jerked back and glanced down at her. "Is that verbatim?"

She lifted one slim shoulder. "More or less."

Luke threw his head back and laughed. A warmth curled in her stomach at the rich sound. "You're priceless, Counselor." His arm contracted, pulling her close again.

The heat of his body surrounded her, cushioning her, making her feel safe and relaxed.

"What are we going to do now, Luke?"

She wasn't aware she'd called him by his first name, but he put his lips by her ear and said, "I like how my name sounds on your lips."

A bolt of sizzling electricity shot through her, making her knees weak. She glanced up and was captured by the dark promise in his eyes. Her heart pounded so hard, she was afraid she might have a heart attack right there on the dance floor. She licked her dry lips.

"Do that again, Counselor, and we'll give our friends over there the real thing, and there won't be any pretending on my part."

The idea of Luke making love to her was a tempting thought. No, it was more than tempting. It was a want that could easily turn into a need. A need that, if she gave in to it, would drive her with merciless intensity. Hadn't she seen her mother ruled by her emotions? When her father had turned to another woman, her mother, Mary, had turned to alcohol to blunt the pain of her broken heart.

If she didn't want to end up like her mother, she couldn't give in to this burning need for Luke.

"What do we do now?" Her voice was shaky, but at least she could speak.

"I don't know."

His answer shocked her. "You're the trained investigator, not me. You should know what our next move should be."

The pianist moved into another slow song.

"Well, I don't. You got any bright ideas, seeing as it was your idea to follow Gail?"

"How was I to know Allen would show up?"

He gave her a see-I-told-you-you-would-get-into-trouble look.

"All right, I'll give you that things have gone a bit askew."

"Askew? Askew? Lady, things aren't askew. We've stepped in it, big time." His voice rose with each word.

Anxiously, she glanced over at their audience. She laid her index finger across his lips, hoping to halt his tirade. "Shh, they'll hear us."

Luke opened his mouth and lightly bit the end of her finger. Shock and pleasure burned a path up her arm straight to her heart. His teeth didn't release her finger. Instead, his tongue laved the pad of skin. The heat in her chest burned brighter, hotter.

Luke's eyes were alive with flame, making coherent thought next to impossible.

"Stop, Luke. We can't afford this now."

His mouth released her finger, but before she could jerk free, his hand captured hers, holding it close to his mouth. He placed a kiss in the center of her palm. "You're right."

The man was deadly. She was glad he wasn't deliberately trying to seduce her, because he was darn good without trying. Thank goodness he stopped when she asked him. In that respect, he was a most unusual man.

"Of course I'm right." She tried to sound like her normal, confident self. "Now what are we going to do?" she asked, trying to put tartness in her voice.

He took a deep breath. "Let me think. Since our audience thinks we're on a honeymoon, our next move would be to try to secure a hotel room for the normal—"

She glared at him, daring him to say it.

The satisfaction in his grin told her he was enjoying this. "—after-the-wedding activities."

"If you think—"

He cut her off. "Once we're in the room, we'll wait for a half hour, then leave the hotel as quietly as possible and take the next flight back to Dallas."

She had built up a good head of steam to tell Detective Lucas McGill he wasn't entitled to any fringe benefits on this trip, but he deflated her anger with his line about sneaking out of the hotel.

"Does that meet with your approval, Counselor?"

"Sounds reasonable to me."

The pianist ended his performance and left the stage.

"Good. Then smile pretty 'cause we're fixing to tell our friends goodbye."

Arm in arm they walked back to the table. Luke extended his hand to Bill. "Thank you for the dinner and drinks."

Bill jumped to his feet. "Why, you're welcome, Luke. You two made my day."

"Well, we're going to try to get a room now. It was nice meeting you all."

"You don't have a room?" Bill asked.

"'Fraid not," J.D. answered. "We were a little disoriented when we got here."

A frown crossed Bill's forehead. "Gail, didn't I see a sign in the lobby welcoming some sort of a medical conference?"

The redhead looked smug. "I think you're right."

"Let me go with you all and see if there are any spare rooms. If there aren't, you can have my room."

Allen and Gail shot up straight in their seats.

"What are you doing, Bill?" Gail demanded.

"Now settle down, honey. Let's see if there's going to be a problem."

At the front desk, the clerk confirmed that there were no available rooms.

"As a wedding gift, I want you to use my room," Bill said, his eyes twinkling with satisfaction.

"Are you crazy?" Gail asked, her anger turning her face splotchy. Her strident tone stopped all activity around the front desk, causing people to stare at her.

"What about me?" she continued, unaware of her gathering audience.

"You, Gail?" Bill asked in an amazed tone.

"Us," she said in a syrupy voice, quickly correcting her tactical error. She hugged Bill's arm. The redhead's sudden change of heart was embarrassing. "What are we going to do?"

"I'm sure the kind clerk will be happy to check around the other hotels and find us a room."

"But our things—"

There was a curious note of desperation in Gail's voice.

"Have you unpacked?"

She glanced nervously at Allen. "No."

Luke, J.D. could see, focused in on the exchange.

"Then the solution is easy. We'll just have a bell-hop go up with our wedding couple and retrieve our luggage."

It didn't seem right to J.D. to steal Bill Frank's room. He'd been forthcoming with them—a pleasure when compared to Allen's obnoxious behavior and Gail's juvenile tantrum. "That's very generous of you, Bill, but—"

"We'll be delighted to accept." Luke's arm was around her waist, his fingers digging into her side, sending a silent warning to shut up and not say another word. She didn't know why Luke wanted Bill's room, but once they were alone, he'd have a lot of explaining to do.

"Good." Bill crossed his arms over his chest. "I'll send up a bottle of champagne." He winked at Luke. "Happy trails, partner."

Bill's heart might be in the right place. Too bad his mind wasn't, J.D. thought. Bill was a male chauvinist, deluxe.

As they walked out of the lobby to the elevators, J.D. noticed the panicked look that passed from Gail to Allen.

Something was going on. The question was, what?

Chapter 10

The instant the door closed behind the bellhop, Luke raised his finger to his lips, warning J.D. to keep silent.

"Why don't I turn on the radio and we can finish the dance we started downstairs."

J.D. opened her mouth, and Luke knew she was going to let him have it for his maneuvering downstairs. He had to stop her before she said anything. He leaped forward covering her lips with his hand.

"Shh. The room is probably bugged," he whispered fiercely, hoping she'd listen to him instead of throwing him onto the floor with some judo move.

Her eyes wide, J.D. nodded her head. Slowly he moved his hand away. When he was sure she wouldn't speak, he went to the nightstand and tuned in a soft music radio station. Once the strains of an old Barry Manilow song filled the room, he returned to her side.

"Now what?" she softly asked him.

"I need to check the room for bugs."

J.D. watched as Luke checked the lamps, behind pictures, under the edges of furniture. Feeling foolish standing like a mannequin in the center of the room, she sat down on the edge of the king-size bed. The mattress shifted in ripples, making J.D. grin at the thought of Bill and Gail tackling the waterbed.

The room was decorated by the same tasteless individual who did the lobby. The carpet was red, the bedspread was metallic gold, the pictures were of matadors and flamenco dancers.

As her gaze wandered over the room, J.D. noticed an odd reflection among the cushions in the overstuffed chair by the bed. Curious, she picked up one of the pillows. She swallowed hard as she looked down at the concealed camcorder.

"Luke, darling." She wanted her conversation to sound normal to anyone listening. Glancing over her shoulder, she saw Luke pause in checking a painting. She crooked her finger.

When he was by her side, she pointed to the video camera. Luke squatted by the chair. From the angle at which the camera was set up, it would capture any activity that occurred on the bed.

J.D. stepped forward and carefully returned the pillow to its original place. "That's how I found it."

A knock at the door caused her to jump.

"Who is it?" Luke called out, his hand automatically going to his waist for his revolver.

"Room service."

"The champagne," J.D. said, breathing a sigh of relief. She took a step toward the door. Luke held up his hand.

He peeked through the security peephole in the door. When he was satisfied that it really was room service, he holstered his gun and opened the door. After directing the man to place the bottle on the table, Luke reached for his wallet. He frowned at the two dollars staring back at him.

Quietly, J.D. pulled a twenty from her purse and handed it to the bellman.

"Thank you, ma'am," he said smiling. He pulled the door closed behind him.

That she had money and he didn't only pointed up to Luke how very different his and J.D.'s backgrounds were. He came from middle-class farmers. She came from a rich oil baron. "You're a generous woman."

She threw her purse on the bed. "Everyone's got to make a living." She said it honestly, as if she had respect for anyone working for a living. She was an amazingly complex woman who fascinated him. And if he didn't pull back, that fascination was going to be his downfall. But at the moment, all he wanted to do was lay her down on that bed and make slow and thorough love to her.

His eyes locked with hers, and a charged current flowed between them.

What the hell was he doing here in this room with her? He should be back in Dallas investigating something like a murder or an assault.

Don't try to figure it out now, old boy. Just keep on operating on instinct until you're on that plane heading home. You can keep it together that long, he assured himself.

He turned away from her and went into the bathroom. After checking for any listening devices, he pulled the drain closed on the tub and turned on the taps. Like a cat, curious about everything going on around her, J.D. appeared at the door. He motioned her inside, then closed the door.

She didn't flinch, object or question him, but the look in her eyes told him he better have a good reason for his actions.

"We need to leave. I don't think either Gail or Allen trusts us. And they'll be worried sick that we're going to find their nasty little surprise in this room. So the sooner we get on a plane to Dallas, the better."

"Do you think Bill had any idea that he was going to be the next star of Gail's home movies?"

"Hard to say. Bill's pretty shrewd. Maybe he discovered what Gail was up to and saw a way out by giving us the room. We can sort it all out once we're out of here." He grasped her shoulders. "You ready?"

She took a deep, fortifying breath. "Yes. Lead the way, Detective. I'll be right behind you."

He turned off the water. "We don't want the people on the floor below complaining about water dripping through the ceiling."

They made their way quietly down to the hall, but instead of heading to the elevators, Luke went the opposite way, toward the stairs. When he pushed open the door and motioned J.D. ahead of him, she gave him a blank look. He grabbed her wrist and jerked her onto the cement landing.

"What do you think you're doing?" J.D. asked.

"Leaving." He walked down several steps. J.D. didn't move. Pausing, he glanced over his shoulder. "C'mon, Counselor. It's a ways down to the first floor."

"Yeah, try seventeen floors, McGill. I've got on heels. I won't be able to walk by the time I get to the bottom."

Resting his hands on his hips, he shook his head. Amazing. Ms. Determination was balking at racing down a measly seventeen flights of stairs. No matter that they were cold, steep and concrete. If it had suited her, J.D. would've thrown her shoes away and run down the steps barefoot. "Well, then take them off."

"You're going to insist on this, aren't you?"

There was a strange note in her voice that caught his attention. He turned and faced her. "Is something wrong?"

"No, why would you think that?"

"Because you're stalling, Counselor. I'm not doing this simply to be disagreeable. We need to slip out of this place unnoticed. Who'd believe we would take the stairs down from the seventeenth floor?"

"Yeah, who?"

"Quit complaining, J.D. I'm not the one who insisted on coming to Vegas."

That put the starch in her backbone. She pulled off her shoes and threw them into her purse. "You're going to keep harping on that, aren't you, McGill," she grumbled, walking by him. "How else would you have discovered Gail was blackmailing Bill? And how else would we have guessed that my ex-husband might be involved in this mess up to his eyebrows?"

He trudged after her. "By simple, foot-pounding police work. The price wouldn't have been as high."

She stopped dead on the steps. He plowed into her, knocking her down a step onto a landing. She stumbled but was able to keep her balance. As soon as she steadied herself, she turned on him.

"Listen, McGill, today was no picnic for me. Not only did I find myself railroaded into marrying you, but the one person in the entire universe that I wouldn't want within a hundred miles of me was there to witness it. In addition to that, I had to put up with Gail's harping, your I-told-you-so attitude, and now I have to climb down this living tomb in bare feet. The first thing I'll do tomorrow morning is file annulment papers. Happy?"

She didn't wait for an answer but whirled and hurried down the next flight of stairs.

Well, she told you, didn't she? And don't you feel like a big man, dumping on her? In that moment, he felt he'd given Allen a run for his money to see who was the biggest jerk.

By the time they reached the ground floor, Luke's knees were aching. Never again would he stay in a room above the first floor.

"Now what?" J.D. asked, not bothering to open the door to the hall, as they stood in the stairwell. He noted she carefully avoided looking at him.

"We pray there's an exit down this hall."

She motioned for him to proceed. "If there isn't, McGill, I have no intention of walking back up those stairs. I'm going straight through the lobby, come hell or Allen."

"If there isn't an exit, I'll be happy to escort you through hell."

"You've already done that," she mumbled as he pushed past her into the hall.

He couldn't help the grin. He liked her sassy and was thankful her spunk had returned. A few feet from the stairs was a hall that led to the pool area. He gave her the thumbs-up signal. "I told you."

The hot outside air hit them like a blast from a furnace. The pool area, bathed in red and gold from the setting sun, was crowded with bikini-clad woman and men. Luke and J.D. drew a few curious looks, but most people ignored them.

They picked their way through the dozens of cars in the parking lot to the front of the building. Luke hailed a cab and immediately a taxi stopped before them. As they climbed into the back seat, Luke searched the hotel entrance to make sure they hadn't been seen. He didn't spot anyone, but as they pulled away from the hotel, his sixth sense told him they hadn't made a clean getaway.

Luke turned his back to the newsstand where J.D. was buying some candy and scanned the terminal building, searching.

"What are you looking for, McGill?" J.D. asked, throwing the change and mints into her purse.

"What makes you think I'm looking for anything?"

She sighed. "Isn't it a little late to start fibbing to me? I thought we'd passed that stage."

A shiver slid down Luke's back. It was spooky how she could read him. Normally, people complained that he had a poker face that gave nothing away. With J.D. it was like he was an open book she easily read.

"I was just making sure we weren't followed."

A frown crossed her brow. "Do you think we were?"

He pulled her toward their gate. He didn't want to miss this flight. "I have no evidence that we were."

"But—"

Luke clamped his teeth around the curse on the tip of his tongue. The woman had picked up on his ambivalence. Ten to one no one else on earth would have. "The back of my neck itches."

She stopped and stared at him. "What?"

He slipped his arm around her shoulders and urged her forward. "I think someone saw us leave the hotel. I have no proof, but when something's not right, the back of my neck itches. The only reason I can come up with is that we had a witness to our departure."

He expected her to make some less-than-flattering comment about his feeling. Instead, she looked up at him with grave eyes.

"For once, McGill, I hope you're wrong."

He hoped so, too.

"Would you like a cocktail?" the flight attendant asked Luke.

Boy, would he, but he couldn't afford to have alcohol dull his senses until he had J.D. safely tucked away in her house. "Just some coffee."

"And you, ma'am?"

"Anything with caffeine in it," J.D. answered.

"Hot or cold?" the stewardess asked.

"Cold." J.D. rummaged through her purse and pulled out the mints she'd bought at the airport. She offered him one.

He shook his head. It was quite a blow to his manly pride having J.D. pay their cab fare and for plane tickets. It didn't matter that he had been caught unawares by this little side trip to Vegas. Why, if he had known he was going to get married this morning when he got up, he would've gone by the money machine and withdrawn some cash.

Married.

The word went off in his brain like a forty-pound mortar shell.

Married. And whom had he vowed to love and cherish? J.D. Anderson. Defense lawyer, the Terminator, a bona fide liberal and the most aggravating female ever created. But, he had to admit, she was also gorgeous, with a figure that made most men drool, and waist-length hair that fed unbelievable fantasies.

And you're really fantasizing if you think she'll let you within arm's reach. And yet, each time he'd kissed her, she'd kissed him back with an intensity that made his blood race.

A satisfied grin lifted the corners of his mouth. Who would've ever believed that he, Lucas McGill, Dallas homicide detective, could fire the good counselor's passions? Certainly no one on the Dallas police force.

And it would stay that way.

"What are you grinning about, McGill?" she asked, finishing the last of her mints. One thing he could say about chocolate, it made J.D. more agreeable.

"It's been a monumental day."

She looked at him. The expression on her beautiful face said that he had to be kidding. Suddenly, she started laughing. "McGill, it's been a day straight out of hell. And we've been keeping company with the devil."

"Oh, so you don't consider *me* the devil anymore?"

"I never considered you one. Stubborn, irritating, a royal pain for my clients, but I can say this about you, McGill—you're honest. Honest in your likes, dislikes, your dealings with people. You're nothing like my ex-husband."

"And what's he like?"

"Slime."

He wanted to question her further. What had that exchange between her and Allen about gambling away rent money meant? Why had she asked about Allen continuing law school? What was behind the venom Luke felt between the two of them? Judging from the stony look on her face, he wasn't going to have his questions answered today.

Maybe that was better. He didn't need to know any more about J.D than he already knew, because that would mean he might start to care about her, and he didn't want that.

Still, he couldn't deny he'd like to consummate their wedding vows. *Quit thinking with your hormones, McGill, and start thinking with your brain.*

Good, solid advice. Too bad his body wasn't following through on it.

Staring out the window into the stormy night, Luke's mind replayed their escape. He was almost sure they'd been observed, but he couldn't pinpoint the reason he felt that way.

Something else was bothering him. He stole a glance at J.D., who was flipping through the airline magazine. For an instant on the stairs, she had frozen up. He'd seen the moment of panic in her eyes. She'd recovered quickly, but her reaction had surprised him.

"Mind if I ask a question?"

She raised her chin, and her blue eyes were as warm as an iceberg. "What?"

"Why did you balk at walking down those stairs at the hotel?"

The chill melted from her face. "Oh, that. You noticed, did you?"

"Remember, I'm the trained detective. I pick up on these subtle things."

She laughed and shook her head. "Sometimes, Luke, the level of subtlety needed with you is a baseball bat to the side of your head."

"Which, no doubt, you would be willing to wield."

She gave him a pleased smile.

"We're drifting away from the question, Counselor."

She shrugged. "I tried."

He said nothing, but waited for her to collect her thoughts.

"It's not a very dramatic story. I hate concrete stairwells. The chill in them, the empty echoes, remind me of the fallout shelter my father built in the mid-fifties."

Mid-fifties? Why, she would've been only—

"I know what you're thinking, and you're right. When the big nuclear scare happened in the fifties, I was a baby, but my mother insisted my father build a fallout shelter. Eventually we used it during tornado season. Mother was deathly afraid of storms. Every time a big storm moved through Midland, she would make us go to the shelter."

With her fingers, J.D. demolished the corner of the magazine. "One day a bad storm came up quickly and we took cover in the shelter. A tornado came through and destroyed part of our house. But it also uprooted a tree and jammed it up against the shelter door. Dad had been out in the fields checking on a drilling crew and it was hours before he could get home and free us." She was silent for a long time. "Mother didn't handle it well."

It was more what she didn't say that let Luke know that J.D.'s mother must have cried, screamed and pounded on the door until she couldn't speak. Something just like that had happened in his small hometown in Northwest Texas.

Her head slumped back against the seat. "Ouch," she grumbled, her fingers flying to the back of her head. Much to his disappointment, she had put her hair back into a bun, securing it with her large barrette. It seemed the lady lawyer objected to going around with her hair streaming down her back.

He pushed her hands away and removed the offending hair ornament. His fingers brushed against the muscles at the back of her neck. They were strung so tight, he was surprised she wasn't complaining of a headache. Automatically, he began to massage the tension away.

She sighed. The soft, breathy sound combined with the luxuriant feel of her hair in his hands made his heart pound.

"Oh, you're good."

He nearly jumped out of his skin. He could imagine her saying that to him in a much different setting.

"After that," she said in a detached voice, "I refused to go to the shelter."

And probably had no end of grief because of it. "Yeah, I know how you feel. My grandparents lived just across the border in New Mexico. When there were bad storms, Granny made us all get in the vegetable cellar. Nothing like spending the night between burlap bags of onions and potatoes."

That brought a spark of life to her eyes.

"So you're a farm boy?" Her gaze roved over him as if seeing him for the first time.

"Yeah, but I always wanted to be a cop. My dad knew I wasn't a farmer and encouraged me to go into law enforcement. When I graduated from high school, I came to Dallas and enrolled in the academy."

"You spent most of your life as a policeman."

"Twenty-two years." He was proud of the years, proud of the work he'd done. It showed in his voice, and he knew it.

"Did you meet your wife in Dallas?"

Where had that question come from? He'd just been trying to comfort her and suddenly he felt like he was on the witness stand. Before he could answer, the plane dropped sharply. He felt as if he'd left his stomach several hundred feet above them.

The pilot immediately came on the intercom. "Ladies and gentlemen, there is a large, violent storm system in front of us. Air traffic control has routed us around it. That means we'll arrive in Dallas forty minutes late. I hope this won't inconvenience any of you."

Luke welcomed the distraction. He didn't want to talk about his ex-wife, Kay. And especially not to J.D.

"I hope you don't have any hot dates tonight, McGill, because you're not going to make it in time if you do."

Luke breathed a sigh of relief. Either J.D. had forgotten she'd asked about his wife or she'd decided not to pursue the subject. Somehow he knew it was the latter. Well, he'd go along with the lady. "I'm lucky. I have nothing planned. Besides, it might be kind of hard to explain my brand-new wife to a girlfriend. That sort of news tends to take the romance out of the evening."

"Oh, I don't know. Allen never had much trouble doing it." J.D. wanted to snatch the words back as soon as they were out of her mouth.

Luke met her eyes, and silently they made a deal. No discussion of ex-mates. He wouldn't ask about Allen. She wouldn't ask about his wife.

"Since we have some extra time, let's see if we can piece together what we know so far in this investigation," Luke said, pulling his notepad from the inside pocket of his jacket.

"Okay."

"Gwen's murdered, presumably to stop her from revealing the blackmail scheme she has been involved with. Her ex-fiancé, Hal Weston, is a major player in this nasty little drama. He and Gwen have recently broken up. The parting wasn't peaceful, according to Hal's partner."

"Gail's also mixed up in the dirty dealing," J.D. added. "She's had someone taking pictures—and probably videos—of her amorous adventures."

"From his appearance in Vegas, Allen is the obvious choice of an accomplice." The muscles of Luke's face tensed, emphasizing his jutting cheekbones. The corners of his mouth turned down and the brackets on each side of his lips seemed deeper.

He had an unbelievably sensuous mouth. Great to look at, even better to kiss.

"J.D.?"

His voice stopped her mental inventory. "What?"

"Do you have any opinions on my supposition about Allen?"

"I think you're right. Allen would do anything, sell anything, be anything if it brought him money or furthered his career."

"And you married him?"

"Meaning what, McGill?"

"Meaning that for a woman as sharp and bright as you, I can't ever imagine you getting involved with someone like him."

She should've been angry with him for his insightful analysis of the major error of her life. Instead, what she heard was admiration for the woman she was now. "We're all entitled to one mistake in our lifetime. I just happened to make mine on a grander scale than most people."

He leaned close and whispered, "Do you do everything on a grander scale?"

"Wouldn't you like to know. Now, let's get back to Gwen's murder."

They sorted through each thing they knew and came to the conclusion that Gwen had more evidence of the blackmailing than what they'd found. The killer knew she had it and had tried to retrieve it. He'd failed.

"Do you think the murder was done by someone Gwen knew, or do you think it was a hired job?" J.D. asked.

"It was a neat, professional job."

"Which means?"

"It means that any one of the suspects could've hired a hit man. Or Allen, or Hal, or some unknown man involved in the crime could have killed her. All we know for sure is the killer is a man."

They fell silent, each trying to fit the pieces of the puzzle together. The remainder of the flight was bumpy. J.D. nearly kissed the ground the moment she stepped into the terminal building. She strode out into the night and hailed a cab.

"What do you think you're doing?" The annoyance in his voice clued her in he was upset with her.

"Getting a cab to go home," she told him in a reasonable voice.

"I brought you, J.D. I'll take you home."

A cab stopped in front of them. The driver jumped out. "You called a taxi?"

Before she could speak, Luke stepped forward. "I'll take the lady home."

"Luke, it's been a long day. I just thought I'd save you an extra trip."

"Thank you for thinking about me, but I'm not the kind of man who would just walk off and leave a woman at the airport."

"You act like I'm challenging your manhood." It hit her then that that was exactly the way he was viewing it. She should tell him to quit acting like some romantic hero, but what the hay—if he took her home, she could close her eyes and give in to the bone-crushing tiredness she felt. "Okay, you can take me home."

In spite of her weariness, she didn't sleep on the drive from the airport. Instead, with her eyes closed, she was more aware of Luke than if she'd been staring at him. Each time he moved, she heard the rustle of his clothing. His warmth, his energy, didn't diminish in the quiet. It was a living, breathing thing that curled around her, making her wish he'd stay with her once they got to her house.

As the day progressed, it had taken on a more and more surreal quality. There were moments when J.D. wondered if she had simply dreamed the whole thing. The only thing that had a solid feel to it was the few minutes when she and Luke had exchanged vows.

You're in trouble, girl.

Boy, don't I know it.

"J.D., wake up. We're home."

It sounded too good to be real. She rolled her head to the side and opened her eyes. He looked as worn as she felt. "It's been a rough day, hasn't it, McGill?" She reached out and ran her fingers over the stubble of his cheek.

His smile was warm and inviting. Before she gave in to temptation and asked him in to the house, she grabbed her purse and threw open the car door. "Thanks for the ride."

She had pulled her keys out and inserted them in the lock when he called to her. She turned and took a step toward him. Maybe he had felt the same pull she had.

Suddenly, she heard an earth-shattering roar, then an extreme pressure at her back, thrusting her forward. For an instant she was weightless...then a hard jolt. The ground was rough under her cheek, and she heard Luke's frantic cry before she slipped into unconsciousness.

Chapter 11

"J.D.!" Luke yelled, covering his head to avoid the flying glass. The force of the explosion that ripped through her house blew out the windows of his sedan. Brushing glass out of his hair, he scrambled from the car and rushed to J.D.'s side.

Never, never in the twenty-two years he'd been a policeman had he known such bone-numbing fear as he did this very instant. "Oh, God, let her be okay," he whispered, hoping God would grant the only prayer he had uttered in the last few years.

J.D. lay on her stomach, her arms outstretched above her head. He knelt and lightly touched her cheek. "J.D. Sweetheart, can you hear me?"

In the light cast from the bright flames, he saw blood on the cement beneath her face. His stomach twisted into a thousand knots.

"J.D., wake up, sweetheart."

There was no response from her. With trembling fingers, he sought a pulse at the base of her neck. He breathed a sigh of relief when he found a good, strong beat.

He glanced over his shoulder. The fire seemed confined to the other side of the house. For the moment, J.D. was in no danger from the burning building.

More than anything, he wanted to roll her over and gather her into his arms. He knew from experience that would only put her in more danger. Let the paramedics look at her first.

He looked around to see if someone had called for assistance. J.D.'s neighbor, Sarah, came running down the driveway.

"I called 9-1-1." Her hands flew to her mouth. "Is she all right?"

He looked down at J.D. "I don't know." The words were wrenched out of the deepest part of him.

He didn't have any time to think after that. The emergency equipment and paramedics arrived at the same time, their sirens filling the air with a wail. He tried to stay with her, but the police and fire marshal needed to talk to him. It took all his professional integrity and years of training to coherently answer the investigators' questions, when all he wanted to do was hold J.D.'s hand and make sure she was okay.

The moment the fire was extinguished, he turned to the fire marshal. "If you have any more questions, contact me at work."

With all the windows in his car blown out, glass littering the interior, Luke looked around for another way to get to the hospital. He spotted his friend Mike Frazer, one of the patrolmen who responded to the call, climbing into his cruiser.

"Mike, can you give me a lift to the hospital?"

"Sure. Hop in."

"Thanks," Luke answered, sliding into the front seat.

All the worries and fears that he'd been able to hold at bay while he talked with the police and firemen surfaced, and he again saw J.D.'s crumpled form on the driveway. *Be all right, J.D., please....*

"There seems to be a lot of activity at that house," Mike commented, bringing Luke out of his silent dialogue.

Luke threw him a puzzled look.

"I answered a burglary call at this address a couple of weeks ago. Remember? You showed up."

Luke ran his hand through his hair and came back with blood on his fingertips.

"Hey, you better get that looked at," Mike said, seeing the blood.

"It's nothing. Just glass from my car windows."

Mike shook his head. "That blast must have been something, to blow the windows out in your car. Does the fire marshal think it was an accident or deliberately set?"

There wasn't any doubt in Luke's mind it was deliberate. "He doesn't know at this point, but he's going to sift through the rubble in the morning." *And if I get my hands on whoever did it, I'll kill him.*

"Is she that special?" Mike asked, glancing at Luke.

Luke didn't know if it had been his tone or something in his eyes that had given him away, but Mike had picked up on the concern. "Yeah."

He couldn't admit to more. Not at this point.

Mike parked the patrol unit in front of the emergency door. He extended his hand. "I hope she's okay."

"Thanks," Luke responded, taking Mike's hand.

He tore through emergency like a tornado across the Texas panhandle. Finally, after accosting two doctors, he found the attending physician.

Luke flashed his badge and identified himself. "How is she?"

"There were no broken bones, no internal injuries. She has a slight concussion, a few minor cuts, contusions and bruising. When she fell, she scraped her face, making it look worse than it really is. We would like her to spend the night for observation."

"Has she regained consciousness yet?"

"Briefly. She asked for you."

"Me?"

"You *are* her husband, aren't you?"

If the man had asked him if he was the governor, he couldn't have been more surprised. "Yes, I guess I am."

The young doctor grinned. "Which part aren't you sure of? Your name or whether you're married?"

Feeling his face heat with embarrassment, Luke scowled at the man. "J.D. and I have been married less than four hours. You're the first person to refer to her as my wife."

The doctor leaned close. "If that good-looking a woman was my wife, I definitely wouldn't forget."

Luke gritted his teeth, fighting to rein in his temper. "Doctor, I've been pushed to the very edge and I'm in a very, v-e-r-y bad mood." Luke used the tone of voice he usually reserved for scaring uncooperative witnesses into cooperating. "I'm trying my best to be civil, but if you don't tell me where J.D. is, I'm going to do something we'll both regret."

Luke's words ripped through the doctor's good cheer. "Oh sure, Detective. She's up on the next floor. Room 228."

Luke didn't wait for any further instructions but ran to the bank of elevators. When none of the elevators immediately responded, he located the stairs and vaulted up them. Once on the second floor, he found her room quickly and started to push open the door.

"You can't go in there," the nurse called to him.

He wasn't in the mood for this. "Who's going to stop me?"

The nurse crossed her arms and gave him a hard stare. "I am."

That brought him up short. The woman had a slight build, graying hair and an air of authority to her that couldn't be missed.

"Which branch of the service were you in—" Luke looked at her nameplate "—E. Brown?"

"Army, and you still can't go in that room."

Cooperate, McGill. You'll get what you want faster. He held up his hands. "I'm sorry. I'm Luke McGill." He pulled his badge from his jacket and showed her the shield. The Secret Service must have been giving the hospital tips on how to guard patients.

"You're the lady's husband."

Luke's eyes widened. What had happened? Had their wedding been the lead story on the six o'clock news?

Seeing his shocked expression, the nurse commented, "It's on her admitting form." The nurse led the way. "Have you talked to the doctor?" she asked, pushing open the door.

"Yes."

"Then you know the situation. I need to wake her again. I want to warn you, we can't give her anything for pain because of the head injury, so she's probably not going to be feeling too good."

"I understand."

The light over the bed was on, casting a soft glow throughout the room. The moment he saw her, his heart stopped, then began to beat with a heavy rhythm. He'd been warned but not prepared. She looked small and childlike tucked under the sheets. The bruising around her right eye disappeared into the white dressing covering her cheek. Her lips were swollen and cut. A butterfly bandage held together the wound on her chin.

"Wake up, honey," the nurse said, lightly shaking J.D.'s shoulder.

J.D. moaned.

"Your husband is here," she said, probably to reassure J.D., Luke guessed.

He could see J.D. struggling to wake. "Luke?"

He gingerly took her hand. It was swollen, black and blue, her knuckles bloodied. "I'm here, J.D."

Her eyes flickered open, and in their blue depths, Luke saw her pain. She tried to find and focus on him. He brushed his other hand through her hair. "Relax, sweetheart. Don't try to do anything but rest."

Pulling a penlight from her pocket, the nurse examined J.D.'s pupils. "You're looking good." She squeezed J.D.'s arm. "I'll be back in an hour."

J.D. rolled her head toward Luke. Tears welled in her eyes, then slipped down her cheeks. "Why did they do it, Luke?" Her voice quivered.

At that moment, her guard was completely down and the tender heart of this beautiful woman exposed. There was no brashness, none of the self-confidence that usually carried her through. Instead, he saw a vulnerable woman who'd been hurt and needed comfort.

Unable to deny his feelings, Luke rested his hip on the bed and gathered her into his arms. What could he tell her? He certainly couldn't tell her what he suspected—that the person who blew up her house was probably aiming to murder her. "I don't know," he murmured.

She pulled back. Her eyes searched his, wanting answers. "Why did they destroy everything I own?" She began to cry in earnest.

With infinite tenderness, he ran his fingers through her hair. He closed his eyes and took a deep breath. He'd almost lost her tonight. He didn't know why he'd called to her. Maybe that sixth sense of his had been working. If she hadn't turned toward him and taken a step, she'd have been killed when her house blew up.

And that would have killed him.

With her tears dampening his shirt, her uninjured cheek resting on his chest, Luke knew he was a goner. J.D. Anderson had done what no other woman in the last fifteen years had done. She'd pierced the wall he'd built around his heart.

J.D.'s tears subsided and she drew back. Reaching for a tissue on the nightstand, she blew her nose and dried her eyes. She didn't look at him, and he sensed she was embarrassed by her outburst.

With a touch as light as the first breeze of spring, he lifted her chin. "I'm sorry about your house, but I'm glad you weren't seriously hurt. Things can be replaced. You couldn't." He eased her back against the pillows. "Go to sleep. I'll be right here if you need me."

"Thanks, Detective."

"You're welcome, Counselor."

The last word he whispered as a caress.

Luke stared out the window at the rain-slick street. The streetlight cast an eerie glow over the empty road. In the next hour the sun would rise. He glanced over his shoulder to the bed. J.D. was asleep.

He'd been up all night wrestling the demons of his past, and the devil of his present.

He "cared" for J.D. At this point he couldn't label the feelings anything else but that. Still, the knowledge he had *any* feelings for her scared him witless. Why did it scare him, he asked himself. Because J.D. had the same drive and intensity that his ex-wife Kay had.

He and Kay had grown up in End of the World, Texas, a small farming community five miles from the border of New Mexico. High school sweethearts, they had married immediately after graduation and moved to Dallas where he'd enrolled in the police academy. Kay got bored staying at home, waiting for Luke through the endless hours of police work. To combat her restlessness, she entered college and got a degree in business management.

They grew apart. Different friends. Different goals, different wants out of life.

As Kay started associating with young professionals who were striving to achieve more, she began to press Luke to go back to school to improve himself. Once, at a party, she apologized to her friends when she introduced him, saying he was just a beat cop. It was the last time he went with her anywhere. And after that night, he never slept with her again.

When Kay was offered a promotion, which involved moving to Denver, she took it without consulting him. He came home to an empty house and a note on the kitchen table.

He moved across the room to J.D.'s bedside. He started to reach out and touch her face, but stopped. All his self-protective instincts were going off.

It took him years to get over what Kay had done. Would J.D. find him lacking just as Kay had? Could he risk that again? Put himself out there to be chopped up again?

And yet, he remembered last Saturday, when he had unwittingly shown J.D. a weakness and she hadn't taken advantage of him.

What was he going to do?

Stall.

Luke walked through the rubble of J.D.'s house. Not much was left. Part of the kitchen stood, the outside wall of the front room, but other than that, there was nothing. No clothes, no personal items, no legal files. The fire marshal was back, sifting through the remains.

"Do you know what caused the explosion?" Luke asked, squatting beside the man. Last night he had told the fire marshal there had been an initial explosion, followed by the fire.

"Yeah, I ran across the remains of a bomb in the lady's office." He stood and dusted off his hands. They walked through the debris to where J.D.'s office had been. The fire marshal pointed to where he'd found the evidence.

Luke's expression grew grim. The bomb had been placed directly under J.D.'s bedroom. If their plane had been on time, J.D. would've been asleep in her bed. A cold anger seeped through his bones. Whoever did this knew what they were doing. They wanted both J.D. and any evidence she had destroyed. They failed this time, but Luke knew a person this desperate would try again. That meant the lady was still in danger.

He knew what he had to do. J.D. would balk, but that was too damn bad. Her safety was the most important thing, and no one, including the counselor herself, would stop him.

The pounding in her head woke her. J.D. opened her eyes, then groaned against the offensive light flooding into the room. The events of the previous night came roaring back. They had blown up her house.

She looked around for Luke, uncomfortable with facing him this morning after falling apart like she had. He wasn't in the room. She didn't know whether to be relieved or disappointed. Whatever had possessed her to act like a first-class weeping ninny?

It was simple. She'd been devastated, physically and mentally hurt, and had turned to another human being for comfort. Then, why hadn't she broken down and wept all over the nurse?

Because she felt something for Luke.

But the most surprising part of the whole thing was that he had held and comforted her as if he really cared for her. Wrapped in his arms, she had felt safe and sheltered.

But what would today bring?

As if her thoughts had caused him to materialize, she heard the door open, and Luke walked in. She couldn't read anything in his face and braced herself for whatever was coming.

He set a shopping bag on the bed. He seemed uncomfortable, like he didn't know quite what to say. He pointed to the sack. "They're going to release you today. I brought you something to wear."

"What about the clothes I was wearing?"

He shrugged. "They cut them off you when you were brought into emergency."

She reached for the sack. Inside she found a red sweatshirt and sweatpants, a plain white bra and panties, socks and tennis shoes.

As she pulled out each item, he explained, "I bought what I thought you'd wear. We can go shopping today and get you some more things."

"How did you know my size?"

Much to her amazement, Luke turned a dull red. "Uh, I kind of showed the saleslady what size you were." He waved his hands in front of his body. "She determined the size from my description."

It must have been a detailed description because he'd gotten all the sizes right, including the bra size. If she ever doubted what an observant man he was, this put all her doubts to rest.

Then it hit her. He'd bought this stuff instead of going to her house and retrieving her own things. That meant . . . She closed her eyes against the pain. "Was there anything left of my house?"

"Nothing salvageable."

"None of my legal files?"

" 'Fraid not."

"Well—" She didn't voice her sentiment. Ladies, she'd been told, didn't say things like that. "So, I've got nothing left?"

He looked at his feet. "That's about the size of it."

All the ramifications of her house going up in flames that she hadn't considered before hit her. And panic set in. "How am I going to reconstruct all those cases? Know what depositions were filed? Know what people I have to pester to get my clients' cases reviewed?"

In his eyes there was a gentle understanding. "Knowing you, you'll find a way to do it. I don't doubt it for a moment."

His warm support eased part of her anxiety. His reaction should have come as a surprise, but it didn't. Over the last few days, Luke had shown her a side to his nature that she never dreamed existed. Buried beneath the hard-driving cop exterior was a man who could empathize with others.

Still, she was puzzled and on edge. Why hadn't Luke made some mention of her weeping spell last night? All the other males in her life had certainly taken every opportunity they could to let her know she was the weaker vessel.

So why wasn't Luke making his power move, going into the "me Tarzan, you Jane" routine? The male showing his dominance over the female.

He turned away from her to stare out the window.

She couldn't take the suspense any longer. "Why, Luke?"

He spun around to face her. "Why what?"

"Why aren't you making a big deal about me losing it last night?"

He studied her quietly. "Because I think you did a damn good job holding it together as long as you did. Only a fool doesn't know when to cry."

His words slipped past the barriers she'd thrown up against him. If she weren't wearing this ridiculous thing they called a hospital gown that left her backside exposed and her dignity dented, she would be tempted to throw herself into his arms.

"And are you a fool, McGill?"

A profoundly sad smile crossed his face. "We all don't cry the same way, Counselor. But to answer your question, no, I'm no fool."

Spotlighted in the sunshine, his body was cast in shadow and golden light. Highlights of red danced through his brown hair. His shoulders were broad, his waist trim, his legs long and muscular. He was a magnificently built man. Strong. Powerful. Elemental.

And something elemental, something that had never been touched before in her, responded to him.

"The doctor said you could leave anytime you wanted," he said, rocking back on his heels. "When you get dressed, we'll leave."

The "we" in his sentence caught her attention. "We? What do you mean by *we?*"

He sat on the bed and took her hand in his. "As of this moment, Counselor, you have no home, no food, no clothing. In addition to that, you have no car and if you did have a car, you have no business driving one in your condition. You're going to need some help, and I'm volunteering."

"You don't have to do that, Luke. I can get Sarah or Emma to help me." She didn't want to be his charity case.

"No. I'll do it."

"That's not necessary, Luke."

"But it is." Steel rang in his voice.

Why was he being so intractable? Something was wrong. "What are you not telling me?"

He shook his head. "Nothing slips by you, does it, J.D.?"

His question didn't deserve a response.

"You remember I told you that you'd stir up trouble if you went to Austin? Well, it happened. Your house blowing up was no accident. A bomb was planted in your office. If our flight hadn't been late, you would've been killed."

She could deal with this, she assured herself. Closing her eyes, she took a deep breath. Her bruised ribs protested.

One of his hands lightly brushed the line of her chin. Her eyes flew open.

"J.D., you're still in danger. Once whoever tried to kill you discovers they failed, they will, in all likelihood, try again. You wouldn't want to put Emma or Sarah in that type of danger, would you?"

"No, of course not."

"That makes me the best companion for you, at least for the next few days." He stood and slipped his hands into the front pockets of his jeans. "I've talked with my captain, and he agrees that it is best for you to keep a low profile."

She didn't like the sound of this little plan. "What exactly does that mean?"

"It means for the time being we need to stash you somewhere safe until we get some sort of lead on this maniac."

It was getting worse. "Define *stash* Detective."

"A place known only to me and my captain. And even he didn't know about this place until I told him about it this morning."

She had a sick feeling in the pit of her stomach. "What and where is this place?"

"My house."

"No." The word popped out.

He returned to her side. "Look at the situation through your lawyer eyes. No emotion. I recently moved into a house that I've owned for a number of years but rented out. No one knows about this house. Everyone thinks I still live in an apartment off Inwood Road. You'll be safe, the city won't be out any rent for a hotel room, and I'm familiar with the layout of the neighborhood."

"What about the trio we met in Las Vegas? If one of them is the murderer, won't your place be the first place they look for me?"

"You're right. They'll try my old apartment first and discover I've moved and left no forwarding address. My phone's unlisted and the department files don't have my current street number. So whoever is looking for you will be forced to find me. And that's what I want. I want those bastards after *me,* not you." The coldness in his voice made her shiver.

"You're baiting a trap, Luke, making yourself the target. I can't let you do it."

He lightly clasped her hands. "I get paid to do this, J.D."

"But—"

He laid his finger over her lips. "Even if it wasn't my job, I'd do it. When they hurt you, it became personal." His fingers skimmed her cheek. "Now, no more arguments, Counselor, or I'll arrest you and put you in protective custody."

"Try it, Detective, and I'll slap the city with a wrongful arrest suit so fast it will make your head spin." She couldn't let him get away with bullying her, no matter how noble the cause. She looked down at the ugly tan blanket on the bed and picked a piece of fuzz off it. "Are you sure I just couldn't hole up in a hotel room?"

"The department can't provide you with round-the-clock protection. If you're with me, then we don't have to pay overtime." He shrugged his shoulders and gave her an apologetic smile.

She chuckled. "Ever practical."

All humor left his face. "No. You're in danger. And until we get a better handle on who's behind this, the best place for you is with me."

The best place for you is with me. The thought reverberated through her soul. As much as it scared her, she couldn't deny it. What he said made sense. She was in danger and knew it. And in spite of all her protestations, Luke had the best solution.

"It's a temporary solution, Counselor."

Irrationally, the thought saddened her. "What about my practice, Luke?"

"Let Emma gather as much information as possible, then she can join you at my place during the day and you two can reconstruct your cases."

In spite of all the logical reasons why this solution made sense, J.D. had the funny feeling if she agreed to it, it would forever change her life. For better or worse, she didn't know.

"All right, McGill, I'll stay with you. But I warn you, I don't pick up anyone's socks but mine."

He arched his brow. "Who asked you to, Counselor?" He walked across the room and paused at the door. "When you're dressed, buzz the nurse."

She watched the door close silently behind him. Suddenly, she wondered who posed the greatest danger. Some unknown killer? Or Lucas McGill?

Chapter 12

Luke watched J.D. wander down the wide aisle of the local discount department store. Her shopping cart was filled with shampoo, soap, makeup, two pairs of jeans and several shirts. Earlier, they had stopped by an exclusive second-hand shop in North Dallas that sold only designer clothes, things wealthy women had worn once or twice, then discarded. The saleslady knew J.D. by name and had saved three suits for her.

J.D. boggled his mind. No matter what the surroundings, she seemed to fit in. As she passed the candy aisle, she tossed in several bags of chocolate candies.

"I want to go to the mall next to buy shoes," she told him as they stood in the checkout line.

He studied her. She looked like a wounded kitten with the gauze bandage covering her cheek and chin. He saw past her bravado to the telltale tiredness in her eyes and the slump in her shoulders.

"J.D., I'll take you there tomorrow. We've done enough today."

She didn't argue, which only confirmed his diagnosis.

Luke noticed the looks the other customers gave her, then him, as if he was the one who had hurt her. He felt insulted that these people would assume he was responsible for J.D.'s injuries. The final straw was when the lady behind the cash register put her hands on her ample hips, threw back her head and stared at him like he was a cockroach. He glared right back.

Luke held his tongue until they were in the car. "The old bat," he grumbled as he drove out of the parking lot.

J.D. raised her head from the back of the seat. "Who? What are you talking about?"

"That woman who checked us out kept giving me the evil eye, acting like I was the one who hurt you."

She laid her hand on his arm. "Don't worry about it. I know the difference."

Her confidence warmed him.

She relaxed back into the seat cushions. "I'm more tired than I thought."

For the remainder of the fifteen-minute trip, J.D. dozed. After parking in front of his house, Luke leaned over and touched her arm. "J.D., we're here."

Slowly she opened her eyes and looked around.

He lived in an older, upper-middle-class neighborhood. The small brick home sat back from the street. The yard was well tended. He stole a glance at J.D. to see her reaction.

"It's a good-looking place, Luke. Not at all what I expected."

"Oh? Where did you think I lived?"

She shrugged, then grimaced. "Oh, I don't know. Some depressing place where policemen live. Under a bridge with the rest of the trolls. How do I know? I've never been to a policeman's house."

He wagged his finger at her. "It's always wise to know your opposition, Counselor." He got out of the car and gathered up her packages.

She followed behind him. "Do you do your own yard work?"

"Why do you ask?"

"Because if you do, I'd like to hire you to do my yard."

A dead silence followed her statement.

She shook her head. "How silly of me. I don't have a house. Probably don't have a yard."

He wanted to lean down and kiss her, offering the warmth of his lips and body as a comfort. Who was he kidding? He'd be offering more than a little comfort—a whole lot more.

He fumbled, trying to fit the key into the lock and balance her packages at the same time.

"Here, let me," J.D. said, taking the key ring from his fingers.

Her hair hung in a single braid down her back. He longed to run his hand over that soft mass. After she unlocked the door, she held it open for him. She followed him inside and came to a stop just inside the door.

Her eyes made a slow survey of the furnishings in the living room. It had a Western flavor, the sofa and two chairs done in neutral fabric. The coffee table rested on a woven Indian rug. Highly polished hardwood floors ran throughout the house.

She smiled at the potted cactus sitting in the center of the coffee table. Now *that* was what she'd been expecting, something prickly and untouchable. That was the embodiment of Lucas McGill.

Beyond the sofa, in what should have been a dining room, stood a desk with a computer and several bookcases.

"You're an unpredictable man, McGill."

He flashed her a devilish smile. "Good. I hate to be predictable."

He took her packages down the hall and set them in the bedroom. She followed him, peeking in the first door she passed. What had obviously been a bedroom had been turned into a gym with weights of every description.

"I'm kind of disappointed. I was expecting some sort of early bachelor or police chic, not this neat, orderly place."

"You mean you were expecting clothes on the floor, dirty dishes in the sink, maybe a rifle rack on the wall and beer cans littering the house?"

She blushed. "Am I that transparent?"

Her question stopped Luke. Was she? Or had he become so close to her that he was beginning to read her thoughts? He shrugged. "Don't worry about it. Lots of people think policemen live in caves."

He motioned to the door behind him. "That's the bathroom." Pointing to the last doorway, he said, "I only have one bed in the house. I'll bunk out on the sofa."

With a racing heart, J.D. stepped into his bedroom. An unmade king-size bed without a headboard dominated one wall. The only other piece of furniture in the room was a tall chest of drawers pushed into the corner. Her eyes met his.

He lifted one shoulder. "I was in a hurry Monday morning. Here, let me get some clean sheets and make the bed."

Weariness pressed down on J.D. The day had taken its toll on her, and she didn't think she would last long enough to change the sheets. "Don't worry about it."

He paused. "You're sure? I changed them on Sunday."

Her knees were shaking, and if he didn't leave this minute, she knew she'd disgrace herself by doing something stupid like collapsing on the floor. "This is fine." When he didn't look convinced, she added, "Really."

"Okay. Why don't you take a short nap?"

"I think I will."

"I'll wake you when dinner's ready."

"Thanks, Luke."

He closed the door behind him.

J.D. slipped off her shoes and stretched out on the mattress. It was a comfortable bed. The sheets were smooth and smelled of sunshine and man. As she closed her eyes, his scent wrapped around her, and for the first time in a long, long time, she felt everything in the world was in its right place.

Odd.

Luke checked the steaks on the grill in the backyard. They were almost ready, and he needed to wake J.D. He went inside and quietly walked down the hall, listening for any sign that she was stirring. Hearing nothing, he pushed open the bedroom door. She lay on her side, her knees curled toward her chest.

In his wildest fantasies, he had never imagined J.D. Anderson sleeping like a babe in his bed. He'd wanted her in bed, but sleeping was the last thing he thought they'd be doing. But circumstances had worked against him, and here she was in his bed, aching from the battering her body had taken in the explosion.

But the bizarre twist to the whole scenario was that J.D. had a legal right to be in his bed. She was his wife. Truth was indeed stranger than fiction.

He sat on the mattress and lightly shook her shoulder. She moaned.

"C'mon, J.D. Dinner's ready."

Her eyes flickered open, and in their blue depths Luke saw a smoldering warmth that startled him. Her eyes closed, and she smiled as if pleased by what she saw.

"J.D., wake up."

"It's too good to wake up," she mumbled, sleepily snuggling against him.

Sizzling fire ran up his leg. He gritted his teeth against the heat, determined not to give in to the urge to roll her on her back and kiss her into wakefulness.

But what she mumbled in her sleep interested him. Leaning down, he whispered in her ear, "What's too good?"

Her eyes popped open and he read a completely alert expression in her face. "Nothing."

As she struggled to sit, he reached over and helped her. Her braid had half unraveled, strands of gold sticking out in wild disarray. The sight brought other thoughts to mind.

"I assume dinner's ready."

Her words didn't penetrate the fog of desire in his brain. "Huh?"

"The reason you woke me was to tell me dinner's ready."

He was acting like a first-class idiot, all hormones and no brains. "Yes. That's right."

"If you'll move, I'll get up," she grumbled, sounding like a cranky child.

Determined not to show her he was rattled, he stood and casually stepped back from the bed.

She scrambled to her feet. "I'll meet you in the kitchen." She didn't wait for him to answer but hurried to the bathroom.

She appeared five minutes later. Her hair had been rebraided and she looked more in control of herself. He'd already set the steaks on the table.

"Would you like some wine?" he asked, pulling out a chair for J.D.

"No, thank you, but you go ahead." He heard the strain in her voice.

Her response triggered the memory that J.D.'s mother had been an alcoholic. He set the bottle aside, not bothering to fill his glass, and made a pitcher of instant tea.

"Thanks," she said quietly. "Sometimes smelling wine or beer on a person's breath brings back memories I'd like to forget."

They ate most of their dinner listening to the traffic on the streets outside and the barking of the neighbor's dog. Finally J.D. asked, "Tell me something, McGill. How can you afford this house on a policeman's salary?"

He cocked an eyebrow. "Think I'm on the take?"

"The thought never crossed my mind. But with the way real estate prices are in the city, this place must've cost you a fortune."

He toyed with the last of his steak. Did he dare reveal that part of his soul to her? Hadn't J.D. shared as many painful things with him? He hadn't used them against her. "I bought this house as a last, desperate attempt to make Kay happy. I purchased it without her seeing it, sort of a surprise anniversary present. When I brought her here, she took one look at it and asked me if I expected her to live in such a small house in a plain, middle-class neighborhood. She never set foot inside. I think that's why I didn't sell it after the divorce. There was nothing here to remind me of Kay. But with the cost of the lawyers and all, I had to rent the place out."

"I'm surprised she didn't demand you sell the place and split the profits with her," J.D. commented as she set her plate on the counter next to the sink.

"Ah, that's the response I would've expected out of a lawyer."

J.D. placed her hands on her hips and glared at him.

"Kay didn't bother with the house because she was so concerned that I would want money from her. She was making twice the amount of money I was at the time of our divorce."

J.D. waved away the notion. "That's ridiculous. Anyone who knows you, knows you never would've done anything like that."

Her response bowled him over. She was right. Anybody who knew him knew he'd refuse money from Kay. So what did that mean? That J.D., after spending a few days with him, knew him better than Kay had after growing up with him and being married to him for eight years?

J.D. sat down and reached for her ice tea. "Do you know where Kay is now?"

"She's working for an international firm head-quartered in Belgium."

"Did she ever remarry?"

"Yes. She married the vice president of the company." He stabbed his fork into the potato skin on his plate. "Kay is big news in our little hometown. Her mother gives everyone a blow-by-blow description of her daughter's success. Last Christmas, Kay and her husband flew in and spent the holidays with her family. It was the biggest event since the town was hooked up to the county generator and got electricity for the first time. Some folks who saw both say Kay's visit stirred more excitement."

He didn't want to be bitter about it, but sometimes hearing about Kay's jet-setting life-style made him feel like the biggest failure to come out of End of the World, Texas.

J.D. reached across the table and laid her hand on his. "You're good at what you do, Luke, and you have the respect of your colleagues. That's success in my book. And I'll bet your mother feels the same."

He read approval and admiration in her eyes. She wasn't just mouthing some platitude. She was telling him the truth. The tight knot of bitterness in his belly eased.

At that moment, he wanted to crawl across the table and take her in his arms and give her a kiss that would blow the circuit breakers on this street and the surrounding blocks. Only her battered condition stopped him.

He gathered up his plate and salad bowl and moved to the sink.

"I'll wash," she said, joining him.

He grasped her hands, turning them palm up. The heels of both hands were scraped and bruised. "Not with those you won't. You dry." He didn't release her. His fingers caressed the soft skin above her pulse.

Her eyes moistened. "That's a first. None of the men in my life ever worried about something so insignificant."

Luke homed in on the words *none of the men in my life.* His heart pounding, he asked, "Is that what I am, J.D.? An important man in your life?"

"I don't know, McGill. Everything has gotten so confused. Legally, you're my husband, but..."

Her answer frustrated him and suddenly he wanted to know what he was to her. "I don't want to know what the lawyer part of you thinks. Tell me what the woman in you feels."

"The woman?" she asked, dazed.

His hands skimmed up her arms, coming to rest at the base of her neck. "Tell me, J.D., what that passionate female buried deep in you feels, the woman who kissed me with such sweet abandon at her house last Saturday."

His finger tilted her chin up and his lips met hers. He rocked his mouth across hers gently before settling firmly on her lips. She melted into him, opening her mouth, inviting him to deepen the kiss.

She was magic and star fire. A burning light, bright and warm, in his darkness. His arms closed around her waist and drew her gently to him. He slipped his hands under the sweatshirt to find the satin smoothness of her back.

He feasted on her sweetness. His mouth trailed down her neck, tasting the flavor of her skin. She threw her head back, giving him access to the pulse point at the base of her neck.

In the distance, Luke thought he heard a pounding on a door. Confused, he pulled back and listened. This time his doorbell rang. He shook off the drugging effects of her kiss, opened the drawer by the refrigerator and pulled out his service revolver.

"Stay here," he commanded. He slipped out of the kitchen into the hall. With his back to the wall, he moved to the front door, careful to stay out of view of the windows. He peeked out the security hole in the door and breathed a sigh of relief when he saw his captain, Al York, standing outside. Immediately, Luke opened the door.

"Evening, Captain. What brings you to my humble abode?"

York was an intimidating man. At six foot three inches, he towered over most of the men in the department and most of the suspects he arrested. When people met Al for the first time, they would shrink away from the bone-crushing handshake and piercing green eyes.

York pointed to J.D., who was walking out of the kitchen. "The counselor there."

Luke wanted to yell at her for not listening to him and staying put, but before he could open his mouth, she spoke.

"What do you need to see me about?"

"Your secretary has been to every government agency in the city looking for you. She has caused any number of headaches, mainly mine. She threatened to call everyone from the president to your father if we don't let her see you. Why don't you call the little lady and tell her you're all right?"

"Oh, heavens, we can't have her calling my dad." A sheepish expression crossed J.D.'s face. "I'm sorry. Emma can be a little overenthusiastic at times. I'll just go call her."

"Do that," Captain York replied. Luke heard the exasperation in York's voice and bit back a smile.

Once J.D. was on the phone, Luke turned to the other man. "Why didn't you just call with the message? Is there another reason you came over here?"

Al grinned and scratched the back of his blond head. "I was just curious to meet the infamous Terminator. Since she married one of my men, I felt this need to make her acquaintance face-to-face."

Luke didn't doubt that York was curious about J.D. When he'd met with the captain this morning and told him about the bombing, he also filled York in on what had happened in Las Vegas. But something else besides curiosity had brought the captain to his home. "And what's the other reason you're here?"

York pulled a sheet of paper from his jacket pocket and handed it to Luke. "I thought you might like to look at the fire marshal's preliminary report. He's even come up with a suspect."

"Who?" Luke asked, scanning the page.

"A pro who lives just outside of Austin. The M.O.'s match. If this is the guy, someone paid him to do the job. We're seeking a court order to see if he received any long-distance phone calls in the last few days."

Hearing J.D. say goodbye to her secretary, Luke shoved the report under some papers on his desk. He wasn't in the mood to go twenty questions with the counselor right now.

"Well, Emma's calmed down. And you'll be happy to hear that I got to her before she tracked down my father in Venezuela. If you think Emma's a pain, then you've never met my dad."

Luke glanced at York. "Trust her, Captain. She knows what she's talking about. He makes Emma look like a pussycat."

York's eyes widened, then he looked at J.D. "That bad?"

"Worse," Luke replied emphatically, remembering his last encounter with George Anderson. He turned to J.D. "Can Emma help you with your cases?"

"Yes. Tomorrow she's going over to the courthouse to see what we can do."

Captain York moved to the door. "Well, I've got to get going. My daughter has a soccer game at seven-thirty." He offered J.D. his hand. When she placed hers in his, York's eyes rested on the torn knuckles and bruising. "It was a pleasure to meet you, even under these circumstances."

"It's nice to be on the same side as the police for a change," she told him.

"Oh, before you leave, York," said Luke, "I've got the name of that soccer camp I was telling you about for your daughter. Let me go get it."

When Luke disappeared down the hall, Al turned to J.D. "Luke McGill is my best man. He'll protect you with his life."

Her brows knitted in a frown. "I didn't doubt that for a minute, Captain."

York nodded. "Luke and I have been through a lot together. He stood by me when my wife was killed, and I decided the only way to deal with her death was at the bottom of a bottle. He put himself on the line for me. He's doing it again for you. Don't take advantage of him."

Her eyes widened in surprise.

"Here it is, York," Luke called from down the hall. "Shelly will like this camp," Luke assured Al, handing him the paper.

"I know she will." He pocketed the paper. "Call me if you need anything," York told Luke. He nodded to J.D., a warning in his eyes, and walked out the door.

The captain's words caught her by surprise, but J.D. didn't think the man had come all this way simply to admonish her. There was more. As they watched York drive away, she asked, "What did he really want?"

"He wanted to meet the Terminator."

She didn't buy Luke's answer for a minute. "I don't believe you."

He leaned down and kissed her cheek. "Too bad, because that's the only explanation you're going to get from me."

With a satisfied grin, he walked into the kitchen, leaving J.D to gape at his retreating back. She hated closemouthed men.

Chapter 13

The nightmare brought J.D. bolt upright in bed. Her scream had barely left her mouth when Luke burst through the door, gun in hand.

"What's wrong?" he asked, his eyes scanning the dark corners of the room. Dressed only in jogging shorts, a weapon in his hand, crouched ready for battle, he looked like a primitive man protecting his mate. He certainly evoked those feelings in her.

She was shaking so badly that she had to hug herself to keep from flying into a million pieces. "It was just a bad dream." She forced the words through clenched teeth. "I'm okay. Sorry I woke you."

His eyes took in her trembling form. He walked to the bed and sat down next to her. After laying his service revolver on the floor, he pinned her with his fierce gaze.

"Liar."

Her eyes closed, allowing the warm caress in his voice to wrap around her. How he could reach down into her darkness and despair and touch her with golden light she didn't know. No one else could do what Luke did so easily.

She was startled out of her mental wandering when he wrapped his arms around her and pulled her down onto the bed. From the top of her head to the tips of her toes, she absorbed his fire, setting off small explosions all over her body. Her heart raced and she heard pounding in her ears. She knew she should send him away before her judgment faltered completely.

"What are you doing?" she asked, looking up at him.

His answering smile was slow and sensuous. "I'm holding you." His large hand cupped the back of her head and drew it to his naked shoulder.

Sensations, hot and throbbing, swamped her mind. "Why?" she asked, her voice muffled by his chest.

"Because one of us needs to sleep, and since you're the one who's hurt, it should be you." His hand moved over her back in slow, heavenly circles.

"Now who's the liar, Detective? If you spend the night in this bed with me, we'll definitely mess up our annulment."

He tipped her chin up with his finger. "You've got my word, Counselor. Nothing will happen."

She wanted to believe him, needed to believe him, but experience had taught her men didn't keep their promises.

He must have read the doubt in her eyes, because he placed his mouth next to her ear and whispered, "Let me drive away the demons for you tonight, J.D."

His soft plea slipped past all the mental barriers, wrapping itself around her heart.

She glanced up at him.

Trust me, his eyes entreated.

Something she could not control responded to him. *Yes,* she silently replied.

His head dipped down and he lightly brushed his lips over hers. "Go to sleep. Everything's under control."

She rested her head on his shoulder and slept.

The dream was more blissful and real than any he'd ever had. The woman was warm and willing, cuddling next to him. He moaned and pulled her closer. Her small hand tangled in the hair sprinkled across his chest. When her leg slipped between his, seeking closer contact, nudging his already aroused flesh, he was catapulted into consciousness. Painful consciousness.

When he looked down at J.D. wrapped so intimately around his body, he nearly lost the little self-control that remained.

Her sleep shirt had ridden all the way up her legs, giving him an unobstructed view of thigh and calf. Through the slit on the side of the shirt, he could see her white briefs. She was a tempting little thing, curled like a kitten against his side. He wanted to stroke her and hear her purr.

And he didn't doubt she would purr. The chemistry between them was too strong to deny. He wanted to wake her with long, languid kisses, his hands molding her womanly curves. But he'd promised her that she would be safe with him, and too many times in her life J.D. had been betrayed. He couldn't bring himself to do it again to her.

He cursed himself for being so stupid for making the promise. But it was made, and he'd live by it if it killed him. And he was sure it would.

She shifted, rubbing her cheek against his chest. He nearly leaped out of his skin. He'd keep his word, but that didn't mean he had to torture himself. He wrapped his hand around J.D.'s thigh and gingerly disengaged her from between his. She protested in her sleep. He slipped from under her hold and stood. Pausing, he looked down at her.

She was such a beautiful sight that he was almost willing to throw away his principles and crawl back in bed with her. No, that would only satisfy a momentary urge, but in the long run it would hurt both him and J.D.

He brushed a kiss across her forehead and left the room.

The sun streaming through the bedroom windows woke J.D. She scanned the room. Luke was nowhere to be seen, but she could hear the sounds of weights clanking against each other and an occasional grunt.

Throwing off the sheet, she climbed out of bed. The noise drew her down the hall to the weight room. She stopped at the door and looked inside. Luke lay on his bench press, pumping weights. He still wore only his jogging shorts, and she watched in fascination the flex and ripple of his muscles as he pushed the barbell out to arm's length and then brought it to his chest again. When he saw her, he replaced the weight in its resting place and sat up. His eyes were dark and fiery.

Self-conscious, she glanced down at the cotton sleep shirt she'd bought yesterday. The bright yellow material was loose enough not to show any detail or curve. Yet the steam in Luke's gaze made her aware of her state of undress.

"Do you usually work out so early in the morning?" She forced the words out around the lump in her throat.

Luke snatched the towel from the end of the bench and wiped his face. "It was that or break my promise to you."

"Oh." The word seemed to thud, like a boulder tossed onto the floor.

Great comeback, she told herself, trying to look away, but found she couldn't tear her gaze from him. He had a wonderfully sculpted chest. His skin glistened with sweat, and she longed to run her hands over the resilient muscles.

Fantasies.

Good heavens, she was fantasizing, freely and vividly. He said he'd teach her to do it. He just didn't know he'd succeeded.

Her eyes wandered over his chest and up to his face. She swallowed hard when she saw raw desire burning in his eyes. She felt as if the ground had suddenly disappeared under her feet.

"If you don't stop looking at me like that, Counselor, I'm going to lay you down on this floor and make love to you until we're both senseless."

The idea appealed to her. Yet she remained silent.

He walked to the door and stopped inches from her. Silently he asked if she was sure she wanted to deny them that pleasure. She gave a slight nod.

He ran one finger across her uninjured cheek. She must look a sight now that the dressing had been taken off her face. He opened his mouth, then shook his head. Without a word, he passed her and strode into the kitchen. "I'll make coffee," he called over his shoulder.

J.D.'s eyes fluttered closed. Was she doing the right thing denying them both? She certainly wasn't doing the natural thing. Her friends would tell her she was nuts for not taking up Luke on his invitation. *You need to loosen up, girl,* they told her. *Find a man and have a good fling.* That might have been right for others, but it wasn't for her. She wanted commitment and love. Maybe she was being Pollyannaish, but she couldn't help it, that's how she felt.

She sighed and shook her head. Wouldn't Luke be shocked if he knew what a dreamer she really was?

When she wandered into the kitchen, he was pouring the water into the coffeemaker.

"It'll be ready in a few minutes," Luke said.

"That's fine."

"While it's brewing, I'll take my shower. Mugs are in the cupboard to the left of the sink."

She avoided looking at him. She was on shaky ground already and she didn't think she could handle any more temptation. After she heard him walk to the bathroom, she retrieved a mug and poured herself coffee.

Opening the back door, she strolled out onto the wooden deck and sat down on the step leading to the yard. It was a beautiful September morning, temperature in the low seventies.

She inhaled, enjoying the brief moment of peace. Was it only last week she'd had a home, a practice, a fairly sane existence—and been single? None of that was true today.

J.D. knew how she felt about most of the changes. Spitting mad and ready to hang out to dry the culprit who was behind the ill deeds.

She took a sip of coffee. But there was one thing that had her stumped. She couldn't define how she felt about the abrupt change in her marital status. Oh, granted there had always been something between her and Luke. The attraction mixed with admiration and annoyance had come through clearly in their courtroom skirmishes. But as they spent time with each other over the last few days, the relationship had changed. The attraction had grown, deepened to an all-consuming need, one that interfered with coherent thinking.

There was no doubt about it, Luke was a brilliant detective, and seeing him operate firsthand had been a thrilling experience for her. Also, through this investigation, he had seen her in action, and from his reactions, he thought she was good.

But something else had changed between them. They had given part of themselves to each other. They had trusted enough to exchange hurtful secrets that had devastated their lives.

"Oh, McGill, what are we going to do? How could we have let this happen? Everything was going right in my life for a change, then bang, it all blows up in my face." Hearing her words, she paused, then grinned. Everything had blown up in her face, literally and figuratively.

Her agitation quickly returned. She stood and walked down the remaining steps to the yard. The grass was cool beneath her bare feet. She stopped in front of a large, well-tended garden. Her brows puckered into a frown. A garden in a policeman's yard? Luke said his father was a farmer, but she got the impression that Luke hadn't wanted anything to do with that profession.

"Why are you scowling, J.D.?"

She spun around at the sound of Luke's voice, sloshing coffee over the rim of her cup. Shaking her wet hand, she threw him a disgruntled look. He was dressed—thank goodness—in a white shirt and jeans.

He waited for her answer.

"I was trying to figure out why someone who had escaped the life of a farmer has a large garden in his yard."

He focused on the rows of plants. "Remember I told you I rented out the house for a number of years?"

"Yes."

"I rented it to a retired couple. Three years ago the husband died. His wife took it hard. The garden was a way to keep her occupied."

"You mean you planted it for the widow?" She was afraid of his answer. She didn't need another hole blasted in her defenses.

"Grace and I planted it together. I came occasionally and helped her weed. In return, I got fresh vegetables and she always canned things for me. When she got sick last year, I did it by myself. I think it helped keep her spirits up until she died."

"That was kind of you, Luke."

He shook his head. "No. It helped me as much as it did Grace. Working with the soil, planting, watching things grow felt good. It was like finding a part of myself that I had lost." He glanced at her. "Now, what do you think the police shrink would make of that?''

"He'd say hurrah that you worked out your own problem without his help. I'm sure he's as over-worked as everyone in the police department."

Luke laughed. "You're right. Sidney would've run screaming from the building if I'd darkened his door."

She smiled back.

"C'mon. I'll fix breakfast while you get dressed. Afterwards, we'll finish your shopping."

After sixty hours of being cooped up in his house with J.D., hours of seeing her, smelling her sweet fra-grance, brushing against her while doing the dishes, sitting next to her on the couch as they watched a baseball game on television, Luke was as close to the edge as he'd ever been.

Each hour the *want* became stronger and his will-power weaker. With the slightest provocation, he was ready to pull J.D. down on the floor and make wild, uninhibited love to her.

Finally, in self-defense, Luke suggested that she meet Emma at the old municipal building where the homicide division was located and work on her cases while he worked on some of his. She willingly agreed. He prayed the meeting would help defuse the situa-tion, because if it didn't, things were going to start popping.

Luke found a parking space in the dilapidated lot by the Police and Courts building. J.D. glanced up at the old structure.

"It's kind of a shame that the police department doesn't have a building all their own. You're like a stepchild, given the old and leftover."

Luke turned and gaped at her. "Has my hearing gone bad? You're feeling sorry for the police?"

J.D. shrugged. "At least they could give you a building all to yourself for your administration and labs."

"I'll recommend you talk to the city council for us."

"Not me, mister."

"Sympathy, Counselor, is only good with action."

As Luke escorted J.D. from the parking lot to his office, he ran into more than the usual number of friends and associates. Each wanted an introduction. Several didn't need any. J.D. knew them from rounds in court. Luke noted the flare of interest in several men's eyes, which rubbed him raw. What was the matter with these guys? Didn't they know J.D. was a married woman?

A marriage only Captain York knows about. A sham marriage, a name-only affair, so keep your head on straight and your temper under control.

Emma was waiting for them in Captain York's office, and the minute she saw J.D., she jumped up.

"Oh, you poor thing," Emma clucked, surveying J.D.'s face. "Who would do anything so mean? I hope the police catch whoever did it. And if they do, you, young lady, are forbidden to defend the scoundrel."

Luke laughed. "No need to worry on that score, Emma. The problem is exactly the opposite. When we catch this guy, I'm going to make sure J.D. isn't left alone with him. My bet is he wouldn't survive the encounter."

"Good." Emma nodded. "It's about time the girl came to her senses."

"If you two are through discussing me as if I weren't here, I'd like to get to work," J.D. said in a tone that made it clear she was not amused with the exchange.

"Sure, Counselor. Anything you want."

The look J.D. gave Luke told him if she got what she wanted, the police would arrest her for his murder.

"We're going to need a quiet corner or room where we can have some privacy. It's not that I don't trust your people, you understand, it's just not tactically smart to discuss my cases and strategy within earshot of the opponent."

A slow smile broke over Luke's face, and he leaned toward Captain York. "We could give her one of the empty cells in the old jail above us." He looked at J.D., pressing the point. "Why, you and Emma can have the very cell that Lee Harvey Oswald occupied."

From her expression, J.D. was not impressed.

Captain York came around his desk. "There's a small office down the hall, ladies, that you can use. Let me show you the way. McGill, stay put. We have things to discuss when I get back."

Luke flopped down on the chair Emma had vacated. What was the matter with him, pushing J.D. like that? Or, for that matter, why was he acting like a jealous suitor? He laced his fingers together behind his neck and stretched. Too much time with J.D. was making him lose it.

"Would you mind telling me what that little display was all about?" Captain York said without preamble, closing the door behind him.

Rubbing his forehead, Luke mumbled, "Yeah, but I don't think you're going to like it."

"Try me."

"I've got a bad case of hormones." Luke shrugged. "Living with the counselor could push a saint over the edge, and you know I'm no saint."

Al settled back in his chair and studied Luke. "It's more than that, Luke. Be honest. I've seen you with other women—hot and bothered with other women. None of your reactions comes close to how you're acting now. I saw how you bristled when Johnson smiled at the lady. I thought you were going to punch him out."

"The man was drooling," Luke shot back.

"Johnson drools over anything in a skirt. You know that. It's nothing personal."

"Well, it felt personal," Luke grumbled.

Al shook his head. "You sure you're not feeling something else for the lady besides a healthy case of lust?"

Luke shot to his feet. "Why the sudden concern?"

Resting his arms on the desk, Al leaned forward. "I owe you my life, Luke, my career. You were there when I needed help. I don't want to see you hurt. Be sure of the lady before you make that commitment."

Luke turned away from his friend to look out the window. "I'm afraid it's too late, Al."

The moment the door closed behind Captain York, Emma fired her questions at J.D.

"Well, is he as good as he looks?"

"Emma!" J.D. gasped.

"Don't give me that indignant look, young woman. Tell me, doesn't it make your blood speed up to be around that handsome man?"

It did, indeed, but she wasn't going to admit that to anyone.

"What's it been like the last three days locked in with him?"

"I've been recovering from the blast, Em. I've had a lot of aches and pains."

"Anything else?" the perceptive old bird asked.

A lot of hot flashes. A lot of cold showers.

"According to Captain York, Luke McGill's a good man. Maybe you should give him a try. He certainly can't be any worse than those lawyers you've dated."

Emma had a point. J.D. nodded at the briefcase on the table. "Show me what you've gathered so far."

The other woman looked like she wanted to press her point about Luke, then shrugged and pulled out the papers she'd brought.

An hour later, Luke opened the door and stuck his head inside. "Time to go, Counselor."

J.D. looked up from the papers on the table. "But we're not finished. Give us about thirty more minutes."

"'Fraid not." He stepped into the room, slipped his arm around J.D.'s waist and gently pulled her to her feet.

"What do you think you're doing?" J.D. asked, slapping at his hands.

"You're redundant. You always ask the same question."

"That's because you are always doing something that is unfathomable and needs explaining."

Luke glanced at Emma. "She uses a lot of big words, doesn't she?"

"She does."

"Kindly unhand me, McGill. I'm not going anywhere right now."

He released her and stepped back. "Counselor, be reasonable. You've only been out of the hospital less than three days and need to rest. Besides, you're looking a little ragged around the edges. Don't you think so, Emma?"

"He's right, J.D. Maybe we should finish this tomorrow."

The concern in both Luke's and Emma's eyes deflated her anger. "Five more minutes, Luke. This case needs action today—at the latest tomorrow."

He crossed his arms over his chest and studied her. "Okay, but only five minutes."

"Bully," she murmured as he walked out.

"I've been called worse," she heard him say.

When he returned, J.D. was standing in the hall, ready to go. She glanced at her watch. "You're thirty seconds late."

He grinned, unrepentant.

They didn't run into anyone until the elevator opened on the first floor, dumping them into a crowd of people gathered to pay their fines and tickets.

"J.D.," a man called from the throng.

Luke heard J.D. groan. Immediately he went on alert.

A well-dressed man in his late forties elbowed his way toward them.

"J.D., I'm so glad to run into you. I heard the ugly rumor that your residence had been blown up. I couldn't countenance it, but from your ghastly appearance it must be true."

Unthinking, Luke stepped closer to J.D.

"It's true, Robert."

"Oh, my. Who would want to blow up your house? Have the police caught the culprit?"

"We're working on it," Luke replied.

Robert's gaze flew to Luke. "Who are you? Are you with J.D.?"

Luke had played this game before in Vegas and he hadn't liked it then. He sure as hell didn't like it now. He opened his mouth to let the twit have it, but J.D. beat him to the punch.

"This is my good friend, Detective Luke McGill. He works homicide."

The other man shook his head. "My, your tastes certainly have changed, J.D."

The polite smile and frozen eyes told Luke that Robert was not one of the counselor's favorite people.

"Indeed, they have. I date honest men now." She grabbed Luke's arm and marched out of the building, never looking back.

Luke did, and he chuckled at the surprised and offended expression on the other man's face.

In spite of her mutinous glare, Luke asked, "Who was that?"

"Someone I once dated," J.D. answered.

She refused to answer any other questions, which left Luke's mind to conjure all sorts of images. Images that left him seeing green.

That night, Luke and J.D. tried to carry on normally. They fixed tacos. While he fried the ground meat, she chopped the tomatoes and lettuce. She still hadn't mentioned Robert. Luke was dying to know.

"Want to eat out on the deck?" Luke asked.

"Yes." She jumped at the chance.

The evening was warm, a slight breeze ruffling the trees. They ate for a few moments in silence.

"I hope you accomplished a lot this afternoon," Luke finally said with forced casualness.

"I did."

It was like prying money out of the city council. "Did Emma have much trouble getting the documents you needed?"

"No." She popped the last of the taco into her mouth, then licked the drop of grease rolling down her finger.

Luke nearly choked on his taco. Their little trip downtown today had done nothing to ease the sexual tension humming between them. If anything, all those men panting after J.D. had only heightened his awareness of what a beautiful woman she was.

Calmly, she picked up her napkin and wiped her hands. "Go ahead and ask, McGill, and get it over with."

Luke didn't bother to pretend he didn't know what she was talking about. He simply asked, "Who is Robert?"

"Robert Lynwood is a lawyer. He practices corporate law. We dated for about three months. When he wanted to go to bed with me, I broke it off. Of course, being the practical man he is, Robert was miffed he had laid out so much money without getting anything in return. I wrote him a check to cover his expenses, then punched him."

Luke's mood had been getting darker and darker until she uttered those last three words. It figured. The lady could take care of herself. "What was his reaction?"

Her smile was one of pure mischief. "He threatened to press assault charges. I told him that was fine with me, but I'd stop payment on the check. He never filed the charges."

His laughter filled the yard. "You're priceless, Counselor. Priceless."

Standing by her at the sink as they cleaned up, Luke's light mood vanished. The air around him seemed heavy, charged with sensual electricity. He was aware of each time she reached into the sink to retrieve a dish to dry. When she took a breath, he felt it, one more twig on an already large pile. When the spark came, he'd burn out of control.

They watched a baseball game together, and for the next ninety minutes, his entire being was focused on the woman beside him. When she excused herself for the night, he couldn't remember which team had won. Couldn't remember his own name.

Unfortunately, her exit didn't relieve his tension. After three hours of tossing and turning on the couch, unable to sleep, he went to the weight room to work off his frustration. If nothing else, this situation was helping improve his muscle tone.

J.D. heard Luke pad down the hall. She held her breath, waiting to see if he would open the bedroom door. Her hopes were dashed when the clank of weights filtered into the room.

She flopped onto her stomach and pulled a pillow under her arms. They were killing each other inches at a time.

She wanted Luke.

He wanted her.

Yet neither had acted on that want.

No matter how hard she argued with herself, she couldn't dismiss the idea of making love to Luke. But the worst part of it was it seemed the right thing to do.

She heard him grunt and remembered how he looked dressed only in the jogging shorts he wore these last few nights. His chest was broad and firm, the muscles across his belly defined with clarity—a washboard effect that always made her stomach do a funny dip when she thought about it. His arms were well-muscled, so hard that the veins stood out on his forearms. His legs were long and lean, sprinkled with brown hair.

But more than the physical attraction, which was a formidable force, was a deeper attraction to the man himself. Although his views on the judicial system varied radically from hers, Luke was a man of honor. He'd kept his word to her. And that, J.D. knew, had sealed her fate.

There was no other course for her. She had to go to him. For once, she wanted to be held and loved by a man she trusted.

She threw back the sheet and stood. Her knees were wobbly, but she wasn't going to turn back now. Opening the bedroom door, she paused to listen. Luke was still lifting his weights.

Her footsteps were silent as she walked to him. He didn't see her until she was inches from him. He set down the hand-weights and faced her.

"You should be in bed, J.D." His voice sounded strained.

"I know." Gazing into his eyes, she read a return of the passion she felt.

"Then go back to bed."

She reached out and lightly ran her fingers over his biceps. His muscles jerked in response.

"What the hell are you doing?" he demanded angrily. "Get back in bed."

"No. Not without you."

He opened his mouth, but when her words registered, his jaw snapped shut. His eyes began to smolder and the muscles of his face tightened. "I hope you know what you're saying."

"I do."

The fire in his eyes burst into full flame. "If I walk into that bedroom with you, Counselor, I'm going to make love to you. Is that what you want?" His voice was dark and rough, filled with the raging emotion he tried to contain.

It gave her hope. And joy. "That's exactly what I want, Detective."

When he didn't move or say a word, she took the last step toward him and rested her hands on his chest. "Love me, Luke."

He moaned, then clamped his arms around her waist, his lips covering hers. The intensity of his passion stirred an answering emotion in her. His tongue slipped into her mouth, caressing her.

His hands cupped her face. "Do you know how often I've fantasized about hearing you say those words?"

"No," she answered.

"Every hour for the last few days." He studied her for a moment, before scooping her up in his arms.

"Luke, have you gone mad?" she asked, dazed by his actions. "Put me down."

"Only if you want to make love here on the floor."

She rested her head on his shoulder. "Only if you're on the bottom."

Luke chuckled as he carried her into the bedroom. "I'm too old for that sort of thing."

"Don't sell yourself short, Luke. You'd do fine."

He set her on her feet next to the bed. Grabbing the edge of her nightshirt, he pulled it over her head. Her first reaction was to cover herself, but she stood still. His eyes slowly traveled over her.

He frowned, and J.D. braced herself for his negative comment. Luke's fingers lightly skimmed her ribs. "You're bruised."

"That's from the explosion."

"I'll kill the bastard if I ever find him."

His words rolled over her in a gentle wave that eased all her fears. No matter what, Luke would not hurt her.

"You're beautiful," he whispered in awe, his hand cupping one of her breasts.

The shocking pleasure of his touch raced through her. Her ex-husband's touch had never affected her like Luke's did. He pulled her braid from behind her back and tugged off the rubber band. With his fingers he freed the golden strands, spreading them across her chest.

"The first time I saw your hair down we were at the morgue. All I could think of was how wonderful it would feel against my naked skin." His eyes met hers, his desire burning away her shyness. "Now I'm going to find out. And in this case, reality will be a hundred times better than the dream."

She ran her hands over the hard muscles of his stomach, over his chest to encircle his neck. "I'm not stopping you," she said, smiling.

His mouth covered hers. His fire became hers as skin touched skin. He eased her back onto the bed, never breaking the contact of their mouths. J.D. wanted to absorb him into her bones. His weight pressed her into the bed. She should've felt panicked or at the very least overwhelmed, but she didn't. Instead she felt cherished.

His hands were gentle on her. "Does that hurt?" he asked, touching the bruising across her ribs.

"No."

His fingers shaped and reshaped her breast. The experience was both exciting and comforting. When the warm, wet heat of his mouth replaced his hand, she cried out in pleasure. He looked up at her.

"Don't stop," she gasped.

He gave her a satisfied grin. "Like that?" He gave her other breast the same loving attention.

In spite of the pleasure, J.D. couldn't remain passive. Her hands wandered over his back, learning the texture. Luke pulled away, and she started to protest until she noticed he was stripping off his running shorts.

He settled himself in the cradle of her thighs. Cupping her face, he forced her to look at him.

"We do this, Counselor, and we won't be able to get an annulment—not honestly, anyway."

"Don't worry. In this state, it's easier to get a divorce than an annulment." She kissed him deeply, then pulled back. "Besides, this has nothing to do with annulments and divorces. This is what we want. Toss caution to the wind, Detective."

His eyes were black with fever, yet he gently rebuilt the tension between them with his hands and mouth. J.D. did everything she could think of to speed him up, to bring this exquisite torture to an end, but he refused to be hurried.

When he entered her in one smooth stroke, she convulsed in a shower of fire and light. Luke called out her name, joining her in her individual heaven. Hearing her name on his lips, J.D. knew she'd been forever changed.

She was no longer alone.

Chapter 14

Luke studied the sleeping woman in his arms. Grasping a lock of her silky hair, he rubbed it between his fingers, luxuriating in the feel. He brought the strand to his lips, brushing the softness across his mouth. The sweet smell of her surrounded him, bringing back to mind their loving.

It had been wild. Incredible. Mind-blowing. But what had occurred between them had not simply been great sex.

This time making love had gone beyond the physical act, and for the first time in his life, Luke had given completely of himself. His heart and mind had been involved, as well as his body. Incredibly, the instant he entered her, with the firestorm of delight and pleasure, he felt whole. Completed. And he knew one of the greatest mysteries of life had been revealed to him in the wee hours of this night.

He was sure it had been the same for J.D., because she hadn't tried to disguise her reaction to him.

The question was, where did they go from here?

She stirred, stretching like a cat. She was an incredible sight, clothed in nothing but her gold hair. His body sprang to life. Lightly, he brushed his mouth over her forehead.

"Ah, that feels so good," she murmured sleepily. "You want to try that a little lower?"

He couldn't help but grin. She was asking for it. He placed a scalding kiss between her breasts.

A startled sound escaped her lips.

"Is that what you had in mind?"

Her eyes flew open and locked with his. "No." Her eyes darkened with her awakened passion. "But since you've had such a smart idea, why don't you finish what you've started."

He did.

The weekend passed in a haze of passion. They were locked in their own private world of joy and discovery. They would make love, eat, sleep, then wake to start the cycle over again. Both avoided thinking about the future.

Monday morning Luke returned to a semi-normal work schedule, each day increasing the hours he spent downtown. He was surprised how much he missed the counselor and often found his mind wandering to what he and J.D. had done in the early morning hours before he left for work. For the first time in nearly twenty years, he looked forward to going home each night.

Progress on the investigation of Gwen's murder was stalled, and Luke didn't know whether to be frustrated or elated. The longer it took to find the killer, the longer J.D. stayed with him.

By Wednesday, J.D. was ready to climb the walls. There was only so much television a sane person could endure. Even Emma's frequent calls didn't help break the boredom. Over dinner that night, J.D. announced that she wanted to go looking for a new office.

Luke set down his ice tea. "Why do I have a bad feeling about this?"

She shrugged.

"When do you want to do this?"

"Tomorrow."

"No."

Alarm bells went off in her head. It had been too good to be true. Their time together had been like nothing she'd ever imagined. They'd been happy. But dreams had a way of disappearing in the harsh light of morning.

Now, for the first time since they'd become lovers, she wanted something different than what Luke wanted. She was challenging his authority.

He stood, and she braced herself for his commanding orders. Instead, he came to her side and knelt by the chair. "J.D., it's still too dangerous for you to go out." He sounded worried and sincere.

"Luke, I'll go crazy if I don't get out of this house. Besides, Emma is having trouble getting all my cases together. I have clients showing up at my old office and going into hysterics when they see that burned-out shell. You've got to understand. A lot of my people are illegals, and when they see that burned building, they think they're in real trouble if the government blows up their lawyer's office."

"That's ridiculous."

"I know that, you know that, but the people I deal with don't know that. They come from places where such things are commonplace. I've got to find a way to reassure them."

"I understand, sweetheart, and maybe I can get off tomorrow afternoon and we can look for an office for you. But you can't move in until I get a better handle on who's trying to hurt you."

"So I can rent an office, but can't go to it until you catch this criminal?" She wanted to make sure she understood what he was saying. "What if you never catch the guy?"

Luke's expression hardened.

She stood so quickly the chair tumbled to the floor. "You're being unreasonable, Luke."

He slowly stood, towering over her. "Maybe, but if you're going to push the issue, that's the best I can do."

He was acting just like her father: pigheaded. She felt his hands on her shoulders. He turned her to face him. "You admitted yourself, Counselor, that if you had an office, you or whoever was there would be a sitting target. You want to put Emma in danger?"

She shook her head.

"Then give me until the end of the month. If I don't have something substantial, then I won't put up a fuss about you getting an office."

Although she didn't like it, she was willing to consider a compromise. "What do I do until then?"

His expression relaxed. "If you need to go to court, we'll find an escort. You and Emma can work here or in that room you used before at police headquarters. The choice is yours."

Luke's arguments made sense. It seemed the man could persuade her with a little logic and a lot of charm. Or was it a lot of logic and a little charm? She had to admit the man was good at manipulation.

But was it manipulation or concern? She wished she knew.

"Okay, you've got until the end of the month."

The self-satisfied smile on his lips didn't sit well with her. "Wipe that grin off your face, Detective. It's your night to clean up the dishes."

The moment J.D. left the bed, Luke knew it. He watched as she slipped on her nightshirt and silently padded to the window. The moon was full, flooding the room with silvery light.

Something was wrong. He felt it in the desperation of her kisses, in the way she'd clung to him as they made love. Whatever had come between them, he didn't like it. He joined her at the window.

She jumped when he slipped his arms around her waist. Her body relaxed against his.

This felt right. J.D. in his arms. He held her, content for the moment to share the quiet with her.

"I'm sorry if I woke you," she said.

"It's amazing how quickly I've become used to having you next to me in bed."

She glanced over her shoulder at him. There was something in her eyes he couldn't read that bothered him.

"What's wrong, J.D?"

"What makes you think anything's wrong?"

His arms tightened around her. "You're a terrible liar, Counselor. So bad, it amazes me that you're successful at your profession."

She jammed her elbow into his stomach.

"Ouch, that hurt." It was a weak protest.

"You deserved it."

"And you're avoiding my question, which is a skill at which you excel."

She rested her head against his chest and closed her eyes. Her deep sigh caused his heart to falter.

"What's bothering you, Counselor? And don't deny it. I felt it in your kisses. Instead of your usual abandon, there was reservation."

"I'm a poor bet, Luke."

"What are you talking about?"

"I mean, I've got a bad track record with men. You've seen it yourself. Allen is the biggest jerk this side of the Mississippi, and I fell for him."

The drift of the conversation was making him nervous. "You had a reason for marrying the guy."

Her harsh laugh bounced off the walls of the room. "I sure did. Allen was nothing like my dad, and that was his biggest selling point. I was flattered when Allen started to pursue me. I was in my first year of law school and still a virgin. To have such a handsome, charming man interested in me was a compliment."

Luke knew in his bones what was coming, and his anger soared.

"I smartened up real fast after the wedding. It took less than two weeks for me to discover Allen had married me for my dad's money and political connections. Allen had dreams of becoming governor one day. But he shot that hope to smithereens when I caught him in bed with another woman. She wasn't even eighteen."

J.D. fell silent, and Luke didn't have to see her face to know she was in pain. He could feel it.

"What did you do?"

"I filed for divorce. Allen told me I could have it if my father paid a hefty settlement. I told him with clear, distinct words that I would have him brought up on charges of statutory rape and ruin him with every politician my father knew if he just didn't fade from my life without incident.''

Luke shook his head. Her father had mentioned the mysterious thing that had happened between Allen and J.D. Now he knew.

"Funny, in trying to marry a man the exact opposite of my father, I came up with something worse.''

He turned her around and brushed a kiss across her lips. She was hurting and needed to talk. He settled her head onto his shoulder and wrapped his arms around her. "Tell me about your dad, J.D.''

"What do you want to know?''

So, she was going to fight him. "When I met him, he made a vivid impression.''

She turned her face into his chest and giggled. The sensation was exquisite, and he was tempted to quit playing shrink and take her back to bed.

"A mild understatement if I've ever heard one. My father is the king of vivid impressions. But I guess it was that drive, that strong spirit of his that helped him overcome his dirt-poor beginnings. His parents were migrant workers. Dad determined he wouldn't spend his life picking crops for rich people. He and a buddy went to West Texas and learned the oil business. The rest is history, so to speak.''

"What about your mother?''

"Dad lacked respectability. Mother was the only daughter of the bank president in Midland. Oh, don't get me wrong. I think Dad loved Mother in his own way. It's just that after twelve years of marriage, Mother had given him only one child. A daughter. Dad wanted a son, so he went looking for a woman who could give him one. When his secretary became pregnant, Dad got a divorce.''

She glanced at him. "Do you want to hear something funny? Dad's second wife gave him two daughters. No sons. I always thought it was poetic justice."

She slipped her arms around his waist. "Does that make me a bad person?"

"No."

"I'll give my father this—once he realized that he was only going to have daughters, he made sure they were self-sufficient. Don't get me wrong," she said, pulling back. "I love my dad and my stepmother. Lenore has been wonderful to me. It's just that Dad mows everything down in his path, and if you happened to be in his way—" she shrugged "—well, too bad. I knew I could never live the rest of my life with a man like Dad, so I picked Allen. The cure was worse than the disease."

When Luke had met George Anderson, he had identified with the man's decisiveness and straightforward approach. And if he felt he shared some of George Anderson's qualities, then what did J.D. think?

"C'mon, Counselor, let's go to bed."

After they were settled in each other's arms, J.D. murmured, "You know, it's not fair if I spill my guts and you don't."

She could always make him grin. "What do you want to know?"

"Tell me about your ex-wife."

She was going to make him pay, tit for tat. Well, maybe it was time to talk about that sorry episode in his life. "Kay and I were high school sweethearts. And looking back on it now, the only thing she and I had in common was that our biggest goal in life was to get away from End of the World, Texas."

J.D.'s small hand moved in a slow circle over his chest, making it extremely hard to think. He captured her hand. "Do you want to hear this? Because if you do, then you'd better stop distracting me."

"Spoilsport," she muttered.

"Kay was happy the first year we were in Dallas. But soon after that she got tired of waiting for me to come home. She didn't understand paperwork and overtime. I encouraged her to enroll in college. Things quickly unraveled after that. I became too stupid, too conservative, too much a cop. I came home one day to an empty house and a note in the kitchen."

He tipped her chin up. Her eyes glistened in the semidarkness. "Does that satisfy you?"

She leaned up and placed a tender kiss on his lips. "Kay was a fool," she whispered fiercely.

At that moment, everything came together and he knew he loved her. He pulled up onto his chest and showed her with his body what he couldn't put into words.

Kay was a fool. Her words echoed in his head. He glanced in the mirror, the razor poised over his lathered cheek. Did she really think Kay had been wrong? Had J.D. really understood that Kay had been ashamed of him?

She's a smart woman, a voice in his head argued. *She understood the implications.* Would J.D. ever be ashamed of him?

No. If anything, the counselor would probably punch someone in his defense. He grinned at the thought and nicked himself. "Ouch."

"What's wrong?" J.D. called from the bedroom.

"Cut myself."

She appeared in the doorway, concern on her face. "Is it bad?" Standing on her tiptoes, she tried to see over his shoulder. He saw her head weave and bob in the mirror.

"No." He turned his head and kissed her on the mouth. She sputtered, shaving cream on her lips and surrounding skin. She looked ridiculous, funny and, with her golden hair hanging past her waist and nothing else on, sexy. "If you don't leave this instant, J.D., we're going to see how comfortable it is to make love in the bathroom."

She wrinkled her nose. "Maybe next time, Detective. My ribs are still a bit sore."

He glanced at the toilet, then at the sink. "There are other ways."

She scurried out of the room, her laughter filling the hall.

As he shaved, he recalled their long conversation last night and the passionate lovemaking that followed afterward. He loved J.D. with an intensity that made what he had felt for Kay pale in comparison.

The feeling was petrifying and exhilarating. Sunlight and shadows. It filled him, seeping into every part of his soul. He was laid open to the warmth. Bare against the cold.

She had told him that she couldn't live with a man like her dad. He had many of George Anderson's qualities. Did that mean she couldn't live with him?

And could he live with J.D.'s drive? Would she sacrifice her personal life for her career, just as Kay had? Could he endure watching his love killed, one case at a time?

There were problems. The question was, were there any solutions?

* * *

J.D. pointed the remote at the TV and clicked it off. If she saw one more game show, she was going to throw up. She glanced at the romance novel on the coffee table but decided against reading. Restless, she wandered out into the backyard. The sight of Luke's garden made her face the tormenting demon that had plagued her the last few days.

She was in love. In love with a cop. A complicated, complex, wonderful cop.

The admission didn't make her feel better.

Did he love her as hopelessly and as foolishly as she loved him? Could Luke live with who she was and what she did for a living?

She was afraid. Afraid of her past blunders, of the rotten judgment that allowed her to marry Allen and date men like him. Afraid that Luke was too much like her dad.

She had tried to tell Luke of her fears last night but knew she hadn't adequately expressed them. He probably hadn't understood.

Wasn't loving someone supposed to bring joy, peace, contentment?

One out of three wasn't bad.

Luke had just finished a report and was thinking about taking J.D. out to look for an office when his phone rang.

"Detective McGill."

"Luke, this is Marv." Marvin Street was Luke's old landlord.

"Hi, Marv. How's everything going? Are you missing your favorite tenant? I bet since I left, Mrs. Ables has targeted you with her cakes and cookies. She always wants to mother someone."

"Everything's fine. But something just happened I think you should know about. Remember you asked me to call if anyone came around asking about you?"

Luke leaned forward, tension gripping him. This was it. "Yeah."

"Well, about twenty minutes ago someone was here asking about you. Ask—"

The line went dead.

"Damn," Luke growled, slamming down the receiver.

"What is it?" Captain York asked from the open door.

"I was talking to my old apartment manager and the line went dead."

"So?"

"I asked Marv to call me if anyone came around asking about me. I've got a bad feeling about this, Al."

"I'll go with you," Al said, following Luke down the hall.

"You don't need to do that, Captain."

Al caught Luke's arm. "I want to. Let me grab my coat and I'll meet you downstairs."

Luke nodded and dashed down the hall. He hoped his fears were groundless and Marv was okay.

Luke looked down at his old friend, sprawled face-down on the floor. A bullet to the base of his skull had killed him. Exactly the same as Gwen Kennedy. Luke glanced at the phone. It had been ripped out from the wall.

"The evidence guys are on their way over." Al squatted down by the body and studied the wound. "We probably won't get a decent bullet out of this one. That is, unless the killer decided two shots were needed.''

Luke walked outside and leaned against the building. Guilt swamped him. He got what he wanted. The killer was after him. Now all he had to do was catch him before he got to J.D. Al joined him and waited.

"This guy's a bastard, Al," he muttered. "I want him. Bad."

It was ten, the late-night news blaring on the television, when Luke arrived home. J.D. was sitting on the couch, her legs drawn to her chest, her arms wound tightly around her calves.

He knew immediately she was angry and he was in trouble. With a capital *T*.

His mind raced and, with a sinking sensation, he remembered their appointment this afternoon to go office hunting. The major error he'd committed was failing to call her and tell her of the murder.

He settled into the chair across from the sofa. Sitting next to her would be a mistake. "I'm sorry about this afternoon, J.D., but something came up."

Her brow arched. She obviously thought he was covering for his blunder.

"There was a murder."

Her gaze remained stony. The woman was unconvinced.

He ran his hand through his hair several times. "J.D., it was my case. The man was talking to me on the phone when he was killed."

She unfolded and her eyes softened. "Who was it, Luke?"

He shook his head.

With a slow grace, she stood, walked to him, then sank to her knees at his feet. "Did it have something to do with Gwen's murder?"

The woman had ESP, that was the only explanation. Or she knew him so well that she could read things no one else could.

"Yes." He proceeded to explain to her what had happened.

J.D. toyed with the rim of her coffee cup. Luke put down his spoon filled with shredded wheat and looked at her. "Spill it, Counselor."

She gave him an assessing look which made his neck itch. "This probably isn't a good time, but—"

Luke groaned, his chin dropping to his chest.

"—when can I go looking for a new office?"

His head jerked up and his eyes zeroed in on hers. "You can't. The danger's greater now, so it's doubly important that you stay hidden. I'm going to call in a few favors and get you a guard."

"McGill."

He held up his hands to stave off her further protests. "Sorry, J.D., but your safety is my utmost concern, and that overrules any previous agreement."

"No." She said it calmly, but Luke knew she had reached her limit. No more pushing. "I think you're right and there is a certain amount of danger, so I won't press for going out to look for an office. But I'm going to hold you to our agreement, which means you have until the end of the month, then I'm out of here."

Her statement hit him like a slug in the chest, taking his breath away and leaving him to feel like he was bleeding inside.

*   *   *

The commotion in Captain York's office drew Luke's attention from the report he was reading. He stopped walking and listened.

"Where the hell is she? I want to see Luke McGill. *Now.*" The last word was roared.

A panicked David Sanders darted out of York's office into the hall nearly colliding with Luke. "There's a crazy man in there who's accusing you of kidnaping his daughter," said the officer in charge of missing persons.

So the captain had met J.D.'s dad. This should be interesting. Folding the report under his arm, Luke strode into the office.

The instant George Anderson saw Luke he jumped from his chair. "Where's J.D.? And what the hell's going on here? I got to her house, only to find a burned-out shell. Then I go to the police and they claim to know nothing."

"If you give me a minute, Mr. Anderson, I'll explain everything to you." He motioned for George to be seated. Luke carefully explained the events that had led up to J.D.'s house being blown up. Reluctantly, he included the part about the marriage. If George ran into Allen, Luke wanted the older man to be prepared for any comment Allen might make.

"Is my girl all right?"

"Yes. She only sustained a few cuts and bruises. But I think J.D. is still in danger. She's at my house right now. Only Captain York and I know where that is. And, of course, the guy who's watching her, Mike Fraser."

A broad grin crossed George's face. "You and J.D. got married?"

Of all the reactions Luke had anticipated, this wasn't one of them. "Yes, but it's not the real thing. We plan to get a divorce as soon as J.D. can file the papers."

George leaned back in his chair and rubbed his chin. "A divorce, you say. Not an annulment?"

The old bird was just as observant as his daughter. No wonder J.D. had to be on her toes all the time, if she was going to match wits with her father. "Would you like to see her?"

"That's why I came to Dallas, boy, to see her." George picked up his Stetson and a large padded envelope from the desk. "Lead the way."

On the ride to Luke's house, George fired numerous questions about the investigation. When Luke exited the expressway, he noticed a late-model blue car following them onto the service road. He kept a constant watch on the car as he made his way through the neighborhood.

"Is something wrong?" George asked. "You keep looking in your rearview mirror like someone's tailing us."

Before Luke could answer, the car turned left onto a cross street. He breathed a sigh of relief. "No, nothing's wrong. I was just keeping tabs on who was behind us. Can't be too careful. Not after everything that's happened."

George fell silent until they reached Luke's house. Luke cut the motor and reached for his the door, but George laid a restraining hand on his arm. "I've got something to say to you before we go inside. Don't be in such an all-fired hurry to divorce J.D. You're a good man, McGill. I like that. And I think you're the right man for my little girl. She might be a bit prickly on the outside, but the girl's got a heart of gold and a sense of honor and loyalty that surpasses anyone I've ever known, including me. Give her a fair chance."

"You might tell J.D. how you feel about her," Luke replied. "I think she'd like to know."

George's stunned expression quickly turned to delight. "By damn, I knew I was right about you, boy. You must be a good West Texas boy."

"End of the World."

Laughing, George threw open his door. "You come from that sod-busting town? Only good thing I can say about the place is it's in Texas."

Mike Frazer greeted them at the front door.

"Everyone okay here?" Luke asked his friend.

"Fine. J.D. and I traded courtroom stories. She's got some funny ones."

"Speaking of the counselor, where is she?"

With his thumb, Mike motioned over his shoulder. "In the kitchen, on the phone."

Luke patted Mike on the shoulder. "Thank's for coming. I'll stay with her now."

"Anytime you need me, call."

Mike let himself out while Luke and George walked to the kitchen. J.D. was wrapped in the phone cord, pacing as far as the cord would allow. When she saw her father, her eyes widened and she stopped talking midstream.

"Emma, I've got to go. I'll meet you at Luke's office tomorrow at ten." Her eyes never left her father as she hung up the phone. "Hi, Dad."

George studied every inch of her. "Looks like you had a mighty fine shiner, girl."

She shrugged. "I strive for excellence in all I do."

George guffawed. "Now I know you're all right. Come here and give your pa a hug."

Once she complied, she stepped back. "What are you doing here, Dad?"

He wagged his finger at her. "Why didn't you tell me what happened? I nearly had a heart attack when I went to your office. I ripped up half the Dallas Police Department trying to find you."

Sighing, she leaned her hips against the edge of the kitchen table. "That's one of the reasons, Dad. I knew you'd make a big deal out of it."

"A big deal. My daughter's house is blown up. Why shouldn't I make a big deal out of it?"

Her back straightened and she locked eyes with George. "It's being handled, Dad. Besides, you were out of the country and there was nothing you could do."

George opened his mouth and closed it again. He thrust the padded envelope at J.D. "Here, this came for you while I was gone. I had a funny feeling about it."

Her brows wrinkled into a frown as she read the handwriting on the outside. It was addressed to her, care of her father's Midland office. The postmark told her it was mailed from Dallas. Flipping it over, she ripped it open and pulled out a diary, a small red cardboard envelope and a single sheet of paper.

"Who's it from?" George asked.

J.D. skimmed the single sheet of paper. "Gwen Kennedy."

"What?" both Luke and George said simultaneously.

"Let me read it," J.D. said, batting their hands away. "'J.D., I'm mailing this to you because I have a bad feeling that something might happen to me. The key enclosed is to the safe-deposit box at Dallas National Bank. The evidence you'll need to verify the things listed in the diary is there. I hope I can tell you this in person and this extra precaution is not necessary. Gwen.' "

Luke picked up the battered diary and opened it. He silently read the entry. He flipped through several more pages.

"Well, what's in there?" J.D. asked. "What did Gwen write about?"

"Our guess was right. It was a blackmail ring. Gwen names names, dates, amounts of money they extorted from different individuals. Allen and Gail are mentioned."

"Allen Danford, J.D.'s ex?" George asked.

Luke nodded.

J.D. snatched the book from his hand. She scanned several pages.

"From what I read," Luke continued, "they were as interested in controlling different senators' and representatives' votes as they were in cash."

"Influence peddling." J.D. shook her head. "No wonder Gwen wanted an attorney. She was in deep trouble."

George kicked the chair next to J.D. "That good for nothing Allen Danford. When I see him, I'm gonna beat him to a pulp."

J.D. jumped off the table and grabbed her father's arm. "No, you're not going to do anything. You do and you'll tip him off and he'll leave the country. Let me and Luke handle this legally, Dad. That way we can get all the guilty parties."

"I don't like it. Don't like it at all."

"But—" J.D. held her breath.

"But you've got my word I'll let you handle it."

"Good."

It was astounding to see J.D. manipulate her father. It took real talent to divert George Anderson, and his daughter had it.

J.D. turned to Luke. "We'll need to get a court order to get into that safe-deposit box. Judge Matthews would be our best bet." She glanced down at her shorts and knit top. "Give me five minutes to change, then we can go to the courthouse."

"I don't think—"

J.D. cut Luke off. "That's right. Don't think I'm going to stay here while you get this evidence. Judge Matthews has a soft spot for me, and with this black eye he'll give me that order in two seconds. With your charm—" she shrugged "—you might get it today, and then again you might not."

The lady was damn good at manipulating him as well as she did her dad.

"Get dressed," Luke snapped.

Her smile sparkled. "See, Dad, how gracious he is in defeat."

An hour later, the court order tucked in her purse, her father safely on his plane back to Midland, J.D. and Luke went to the bank. Gwen had rented the largest box possible, and it was crammed with pictures and tapes. Luke scrounged a cardboard box from a bank employee to cart off their find.

On the drive back to his house, Luke couldn't shake the feeling that they were being watched, but he never saw anyone tailing their car.

Still, his sixth sense told him the killer knew they had Gwen's evidence and would act soon.

Chapter 15

They spent that night and most of the next day piecing together the exploits of the blackmail ring. According to Gwen's diary there were only the four people in the ring: Gwen herself, Gail Williams, Hal Weston and Allen Danford.

J.D. pointed the remote at the television and turned off the VCR. "It's staggering what our four eager beavers did." She glanced at the video tapes and pictures scattered across the sofa and coffee table. "They blackmailed four senators, five representatives, got twenty bills passed in their favor. They even have the heads of several state agencies jumping to their tune. No wonder everyone said how good Gwen was."

Luke rested his arm on the back of the couch. "Are you surprised?"

Rubbing her shoulders, J.D. replied, "I shouldn't be." As much as she'd seen in her law practice, she shouldn't have been surprised at the corruption, but she had this fatal flaw. She believed people were basically good and operated with a code of honor. It disappointed her every time she was proven wrong.

"But you are." He scooted across the cushions and grasped her shoulders, turning her away from him. He began to massage her sore muscles.

"That feels wonderful. You're good."

He leaned close. "You said that to me once before and I had all sorts of fantasies about what you meant."

She glanced over her shoulder. "Are you fishing for a compliment?" He looked like a little boy waiting for a treat from the cookie jar. "Well, my experience isn't broad and the sample is very small—"

He pinched her.

"Ouch. All right, all right. You're good, Luke. Very, v-e-r-y *good*." She made the last word sizzle.

He nuzzled her ear.

"Stop that," she said, pushing him away.

"Why?"

"Because, Detective, we need to determine which one of our remaining three was the killer."

"Or, my dear innocent, it could've been any of the people the ring was blackmailing. Maybe one of them discovered Gwen was going to come clean and didn't want his job and reputation shot to hell, so he shut her up."

J.D. picked up a set of pictures on the coffee table. "There's something odd about these pictures," she murmured, studying the roll of film they'd obtained from Gwen's apartment.

Luke looked over her shoulder at the photo in her hand. "I don't see anything unusual. Allen and Hal sitting in a bar with some man. They look like three good old Texas boys. Why, from the angle of the shot you can even see Allen's boots."

"That's it," J.D. shouted. She turned to Luke. "That's what was bothering me about these pictures." She searched the set, pulling out two more that showed Allen wearing cowboy boots. "Look, Luke. Allen is wearing boots."

"So?"

"So when I was married to him, Allen hated Western boots. He claimed he was too sophisticated to wear them. Every time he saw a man in them, he would rage about how wearing Western boots was the mark of a backwater, uneducated person."

"What do you think accounts for his switch in opinions?"

"He did it because he wanted to make a favorable impression with someone. Maybe the boots were given to him as a gift by a powerful person."

"And I'll bet the boots have a unique heel with the outline of the state of Texas etched into them." Luke stood and began to pace. "Anyone else in those pictures wearing boots?"

She flipped through the photos. "No."

"I'll need to clear it with my captain, but I'll call Craig Winston with Austin P.D. and have him obtain a search warrant for Allen's residence."

"If you arrest only Allen, the rest will run for cover, giving you guys no end of trouble. It will save you all some grief if you take them all in at the same time."

Luke froze and gave J.D. a surprised look. "Why, Counselor, it sounds like you're taking up for the police."

She walked to him and jabbed her finger into his chest. "Detective, I've always wanted to see right prevail. In this case, we know which side is right."

He captured her hand, then pressed a warm, sensuous kiss into the palm. "You mean that if your exhusband asks you to defend him, you'll turn him down?"

She tried to punch him, but Luke refused to release her hand. Instead he placed it behind his back and slid his arms around her waist. "You're dangerous, Counselor, when aroused." He grinned wickedly.

She took a small bow. "Why, thank you, Detective. It's always nice to be respected." She raised up on her toes and her mouth met his. The kiss was consuming, shutting out the world, leaving only the two lovers.

Finally, Luke lifted his head. Regret showed in his eyes. "I wish we had time to finish this, but the sooner Allen and his friends are behind bars, the easier I'll rest." He glanced at his watch. It was a little after nine, and he knew Al York was home. Since Al lived in Oak Cliff, ten miles southwest of downtown, it was quicker and easier for the two men to meet at the captain's office. After the arrangements had been made, Luke picked up his address book and searched for Mike Frazer's number.

"Who are you calling now?" J.D. asked.

"Mike. I hope he isn't on the evening shift tonight. If he is, it might take a little longer to find someone to come over here."

Hands on her hips, J.D. scowled at him. "McGill, I don't need a baby-sitter. By the time it takes you to locate someone, you could be there and back. And in the meantime, Allen is running loose doing heaven knows what."

He picked up the telephone receiver, but she put her hand over the buttons. "Trust me, Luke. I can take care of myself." He hesitated. "If it will make you feel any better, I'll keep the gun you have in the kitchen by my side."

It didn't make him feel any better. Against his better judgment, he let her have her way. "Okay, J.D. Just make sure you know what you're aiming at before you fire."

She kissed him. "Thanks, Luke."

He gathered up the pictures and Gwen's diary and placed them in the mailer.

"What are you doing?"

He paused. "I'm surprised at you, Counselor. I'll need to show this evidence to my captain to assure him we have enough concrete proof for these arrests." He pointed to the videos and other photos. "Why don't you put those back in the box and hide them in my closet."

She nodded. "Be sure and tell the Austin district attorney to request these suspects be denied bail. They'll run if given the slightest chance."

"Yes, Mother."

His sarcasm cut through her worry. Luke had done this thing a thousand times before and knew what he was doing. He didn't need her telling him how to arrest suspects. She moved to his side and touched his arm. "I'm sorry, Luke. It's just kind of odd to find myself on this side of the law enforcement game. I know you'll do a thorough job."

He kissed her with a tenderness that brought tears to her eyes. "Thanks for the vote of confidence. Lock the door after I leave." He cupped her face. "Just think, tomorrow at this time we should have the killer behind bars and you'll be free to go wherever you want."

It was what she wanted, an end to her confinement in this house. Yet somehow the thought was dark and depressing.

At the end of the block, parked between two small cars, was the blue Ford. The driver watched the cop get into his vehicle and drive off. He waited patiently for several minutes to make sure the man was actually gone. Satisfied the way was clear, the driver got out of his car. A cold smile, full of venom and revenge, transformed the handsome face into a hideous mask as he walked toward the house.

When the doorbell sounded five minutes later, J.D. smiled, thinking that Luke had forgotten something. She flung open the door. "What did you—"

She cursed herself for being an idiot and not checking who was at the door before she opened it. She also cursed herself for forgetting Luke's gun, which was still sitting in the kitchen drawer.

Allen's smile made her sick.

Gathering her scattered thoughts, she demanded, "What are you doing here?"

Slowly Allen raised his right hand, and J.D. saw the gun. "I've come for the things Gwen gave you." He motioned her back into the living room. His gaze moved around the room. "Where are they, J.D.? I saw you and your new cop husband retrieve them from the bank. By the way, that wasn't very nice of you, failing to mention Luke McGill was a cop."

J.D. was grateful she'd listened to Luke and hidden the box. "I imagine it came as a big surprise to you."

Allen's eyes darkened dangerously. "It's a minor annoyance, but nothing I can't handle."

J.D. sat on the couch. "Do the others know that you killed Gwen?"

His fingers tightened around the handle of the gun. "Who says I killed Gwen?"

She glanced down at Allen's feet. Her heart raced when she saw the Western boots he wore. Here was the evidence they were looking for. He walked around the end of the couch and sat down. The gun was pointed at her heart.

"Did Hal and Gail know that Gwen was going to turn state's evidence?"

He gave her a who-cares shrug. "Gwen was a nervous ninny. She never was comfortable with the setup. I introduced her to Hal. He was the one who seduced her and got her involved. After a while, she started harping about the situation, getting nervous about being caught. She even started spouting stuff about our moral corruption. Hal promised he could keep her in line, but when she moved out of his apartment, I knew he'd lost his hold over her."

He crossed his legs, resting his booted ankle on the opposite knee. J.D.'s heart pounded. As casually as she could, she looked at the heel. Adrenaline raced through her system when she saw the outline of the state of Texas carved into the rubber.

"It was just a matter of time until she broke," Allen continued, oblivious to the direction of J.D.'s gaze. "The moment she saw your dad at that damn reception, I knew we were in trouble. And I was right. She ran straight to J.D. Anderson, defense lawyer, champion of the underdog," he snarled in contempt. "Do you know how many people I run into from Midland who sing your praises and tell me what a wonderful human being you are? They obviously haven't tried to live with you. And they certainly don't know what a cold fish you are in bed, do they? I've been tempted to tell, but—'' He waved away the thought.

"I'm drifting from my point. I followed Gwen here to Dallas. She must've sensed it because she put the evidence she had in the bank. Then I saw her mail something in the bank lobby. I guessed it was the key to the safe-deposit box. I thought she'd mailed it to you. She certainly didn't have it on her later."

J.D. prayed he didn't realize that he had just inadvertently admitted killing Gwen. "So you're the one responsible for the burglaries and the bombing of my house."

He grinned, seemingly pleased with the destruction of her home. Anger exploded in her head. Allen was still a first-class bastard. If he hadn't been holding a gun, she would have launched herself at him.

"Why don't you move a little farther down the couch, J.D. I wouldn't want you to get too close. Remember, I know you have a brown belt in judo."

Her thoughts must've shown on her face. She knew she'd better get control of her emotions quickly. Taking a deep breath, she moved to the end of the cushions. "You didn't answer my question, Allen. Were you responsible for what happened to my house?"

Narrowing his eyes, Allen studied her. "Yeah, I was responsible."

"You intended to kill me with that bomb." She said the words calmly, carefully, as if questioning a witness in court.

"You and that new hubby of yours. Too bad your flight was late getting back to Dallas. My problems would've been solved."

Keep control, she told herself. "Wrong. You see Gwen was smarter than you gave her credit for. She mailed the key and her diary, which detailed all the deals you made, to my dad's Midland office. He would've opened it and discovered who murdered three people."

Allen leaned forward and rested his elbows on his knees. "Which brings me back to my reason for being here—to get the evidence. Where is it, J.D.?" He glanced around the room.

There was no way in creation she'd tell him that part of the evidence was hidden down the hall in a closet. "It's not here. When Luke left, he took it with him to show his captain."

Leaping to his feet, Allen motioned with his gun for her to do the same. "Where's the phone?"

She pointed behind her. "In the kitchen."

"Call McGill. I don't care how you do it, but get him back here with the evidence or you're a dead woman."

"I don't know the number."

Allen cocked the gun. "Call information."

It took several minutes for her to get the right number. Then she was transferred from one desk to another. Finally, on the third try, she got Captain York.

"Is Luke there, Captain?"

"No."

"When he gets there will you have him call home immediately? It's important."

J.D.'s heart nearly failed when silence was the only answer to her request.

"Is something wrong?" Captain York asked in a low, steady voice.

This was her chance to warn Luke. She racked her brain for something that would alert Luke but keep Allen thinking that everything was going according to his plan. "This is kind of embarrassing, but Luke and

I had a fight. I want to tell him he was right and apologize. You know how newlyweds are."

"I'll give him your message."

J.D.'s hand shook when she hung up the phone. She couldn't tell whether York had picked up on her signals. "He'll call when he gets there."

"Then why don't we sit down and wait for him?" Allen motioned with his gun. She preceded him into the living room and sat where he indicated. Her only hope now was that Luke would understand her warning.

Al York frowned at the phone on his desk. Although J.D. had sounded perfectly normal, and what she said perfectly innocent, he couldn't shake the feeling that she wouldn't have called unless something was seriously wrong.

He stood, intending to go down to dispatch to contact Luke, when Luke walked into his office.

"Al, I've got something here you need to see."

"Wait," Al said, holding up his hand. "J.D. just called."

The mailer fell from Luke's nerveless fingers onto the desk. His sixth sense, which had been hammering him all the way over here, kicked into overdrive. "What did she say?"

"She said she called to apologize for the fight you two had before you left."

That didn't make sense. They had almost made love, but under no circumstances would she construe that as a fight. Unless she deliberately wanted to tell him something. "What exactly did she say?"

Al closed his eyes, fighting for the exact words. "She said, 'I want to tell him—you—he was right and apologize.'"

Luke recalled their conversation. Separating it from the sexual innuendoes and loving touches was hard. "We were talking about getting a court order to search Allen Danford's residence for the boots—" He let out a string of vivid, harsh curses. "What if he's there at my house with J.D.?" Luke ran his fingers through his hair. "Why didn't I listen to that little voice telling me something was wrong."

"Call her," Al ordered.

With each number he punched in, the muscles of Luke's stomach tightened. J.D. answered on the second ring. "Hello." Her voice had a breathy quality.

Keep it light, McGill, he cautioned himself just in case Allen was listening. "Hi, sweetheart. Captain York said you called."

"I need you to come home, Luke, right away. And bring that envelope Dad brought me from Midland." Luke also heard the underlying message. *Allen's here and going to hurt me if he doesn't get his hands on the evidence.*

"No problem. I'm leaving now. Sit tight."

Her sigh of relief came across the wire clearly. "Hurry." She hung up.

Luke looked at Al. "He's there and wants the evidence I brought."

"What are you going to do?"

"I'm going to play along with him until I can get J.D. safely away. Then he'd better pray the backup has shown up, because he'll need the police to protect him from me."

Allen settled himself comfortably against the cushions of the couch. From his smile, J.D. knew he was enjoying his power over her. She eyed the gun. If she could just get it away from him, she could easily disable him.

"You're having naughty thoughts, J.D. Don't do that," he admonished, wiggling the barrel of the gun toward her.

"I don't know what you're talking about," she snapped back, unable to keep the irritation out of her voice.

"You're plotting to get this." He tapped his pistol. "Well, forget it. I won't let you get close enough."

She threw up her hands and looked away. "Think what you like."

"Tell me something. Were you really shocked when you found me in bed with that teenager? Or had you figured out by then that I only married you for your money?"

"No, I wasn't surprised. I was surprised that you were so sloppy about your lady friends that you didn't notice the girl was underage."

"Oh, I knew and found it exciting."

J.D. closed her eyes. The man made her sick.

"What I didn't count on was what a bitch you'd be about the divorce."

The bitter laugh tumbled out of her. "I may have been naive, but I was never stupid, Allen."

"Yeah, I'll give you that. A bitter, dried-up prune, but never stupid."

The knock on the door made her jump. Luke's voice calling her name followed quickly.

"Open it," Allen snapped.

Heart racing, she obeyed him. The reassurance of Luke's presence wrapped around her like a blanket, comforting her. His eyes searched hers. She gave him a small smile.

"Come inside, McGill," Allen called out, "or I'll shoot her."

Luke's head turned and his eyes clashed with Allen's. The air around Luke vibrated with his rage as he stepped into the house and closed the door behind him. He reached for J.D., but Allen shook his head.

"No, you don't. I don't want you two close together. Detective, you take one end of the couch. J.D. the other." He backed up and watched them comply. "Now, McGill, open that packet of evidence so I can make sure you brought the right stuff."

With his eyes never leaving Allen's face, Luke opened the mailer and shook the contents onto the coffee table. The pictures scattered around the potted cactus and across the wood surface.

"Is that all?" Allen questioned.

"Yes," Luke answered.

Allen looked unconvinced until he glanced down at the incriminating shots, then seemed to forget his doubts. "That stupid broad." He edged closer and picked up the diary. He backed away until he bumped into the chair on the other side of the room, then sat. Allen kept the gun pointed at them while he tried to flip through the diary. His eyes bulged and his lips compressed into a small line as he read several entries.

"Fool," Allen yelled, hurling the book across the room. Luke and J.D. ducked as it flew over their heads and hit the wall behind them.

"I ought to kill Hal for being so stupid. He's responsible for this mess. If he hadn't gotten Gwen involved, everything would still be running smoothly."

J.D. saw her opportunity. Allen was upset. If she could push him harder, he might get careless and they could disarm him. "You mean you could still be blackmailing officials in Austin and no one would be the wiser?"

With jerky movements, Allen stood and pointed the gun at her. "You always had a smart mouth, J.D. Too bad that's all it was good for."

J.D. felt her cheeks go red-hot. The man was such an incredible jerk. Luke came off the couch but froze when Allen pulled back the gun's hammer and pointed it at J.D. "Try it and I'll kill her."

Luke slowly sank back down.

"That's good. Now, J.D., why don't you pick up Gwen's diary and these pictures and put them in the envelope."

"Why should I?"

"Because I have the gun."

She walked around the couch and picked up the diary. "Is it getting easier to kill, Allen? After all, Luke and I will be your second and third victims. Or will we be your third and fourth?"

Allen cocked his head. "Yeah, it gets easier. So easy, in fact, that if you don't stop stalling, I'm going to kill your brand-new husband, saving him the misery of going through a honeymoon with you."

J.D. thrust the book into the mailer, then the pictures.

"Slide it over to the edge of the table."

She glanced at Luke. If they didn't stop Allen, he was going to murder them. And she wasn't going to let him do it. She loved Luke and wanted an opportunity to tell him.

"Quit looking at him. Do what I said."

Luke's pulses were pounding so loud that he barely heard what Allen said. He had this sick feeling in the pit of his stomach that J.D. was going to do something foolish, like get herself killed. She was deliberately pushing Allen, hoping that he would respond recklessly. If she'd just wait, the captain would arrive with the backup.

"Do what he says, J.D.," Luke muttered.

"That's a smart cop," Allen told Luke. "Now, let's see if the attorney can be as smart."

The expression on J.D.'s face chilled Luke. The lady had taken all she could. She was going to act, which scared him to death. He prepared himself mentally for her actions, whatever they might be.

J.D. slid the packet to the edge of the coffee table to where it teetered precariously, half on, half off the surface.

Allen lunged for the envelope. At the same instant, J.D. sprang forward and shoved the cactus into Allen's face. He screamed and pulled the trigger. Luke tackled J.D., sending her into the cushions of the couch, out of the line of fire. The shot slammed into the wall above their heads.

Instantly Luke was off the couch and plunging across the coffee table. He caught Allen around the waist and wrestled him to the floor, but not before another shot slammed into the wall.

The front and back doors burst open, and uniformed policemen poured into the room. Allen was quickly subdued.

"Is anyone hurt?" York asked, looking at J.D., then Luke.

"I'm fine," J.D. said in an unsteady voice. "Are you okay, Luke?"

"No," he yelled. "I nearly died of cardiac arrest when I saw you shove the cactus into that maniac. Whatever possessed you to do something so stupid?"

J.D. stared at him in shock.

"Why did you do it?" he demanded harshly.

Here it was, the opportunity to tell him how she felt. She had prayed during those minutes alone with Allen that she'd have this chance. It was a gamble, and if she lost, half the Dallas police force would witness her humiliation. But in spite of that daunting fact, J.D. knew she had to risk it. "I did it because I love you, Luke, and didn't want you to get hurt."

She saw him clench his jaw and ball his hands into fists. "If you love me, then why didn't you trust me?"

The room fell silent, and J.D.'s hopes died.

"I had it under control, Counselor. As you can see, help was on the way. I was stalling until they got here and our chances of getting out of this alive were better."

Words were inadequate. She'd told him she acted out of love. He saw her actions only as a lack of trust, an insult to his judgment that would soon make the rounds of the police department.

One of the uniformed officers took Allen outside. Luke picked up the packet. "I've got to go and make a report."

"Luke." She stepped toward him.

He shook his head. "We'll talk later."

She watched him get into his car and drive away. She'd risked everything and lost.

Chapter 16

She closed the door after the last officer and locked it. The pain around her heart was so intense that it was hard to breathe. Well, by the end of this shift, every officer on the police force would know she loved Lucas McGill, but he didn't love her in return.

Slowly her gaze moved around the room she'd come to think of as home. There was nothing left to do but pack her things and leave. She went to the kitchen and dialed Emma's number.

"Em, this is J.D. The police caught the killer. Can I stay at your house for a few days?"

"That's great, sweetie, but why do you need to stay with me?"

"Can I stay or not?" J.D. knew she'd break down into a crying blob if she had to explain.

"Sure."

"I'll call a cab and be over there in about an hour.

Oh, and Emma, I want you to file those divorce papers for me tomorrow.''

"Does Luke know about this?''

"No. But do it, anyway.''

She didn't wait for Emma to argue with her, but instead hung up.

It took only minutes to pack her few belongings into a shopping bag. Placing the bag by the couch, she sat and waited for Luke to come home. He at least deserved a thank-you.

For the first time, she noticed the mess on the coffee table. Soil, pieces of the broken pot and battered cactus were scattered across the wooden surface, spilling onto the rug.

She reached out and ran her fingers through the soil. Lovingly, she touched the velvety skin of the cactus between its spines. Luke was like this. Once you got past his defenses, he was a treasure.

Even if she couldn't save her marriage, maybe she could save this poor cactus. She retrieved the spare clay pot she saw in the backyard and began to repot the cactus.

It was close to midnight when they finished the paperwork on Allen's arrest. As Luke drove home, he wondered if J.D. was still there.

He didn't really expect to find her. He'd been unusually hard on her after Allen had been cuffed, said things that sprang strictly from heart-wrenching fear. But didn't she understand how close she'd come to death? And how recklessly she'd acted?

He could still taste the terror that had filled him when she threw the cactus at Allen. He'd barely had enough time to shove her out of the way of the bullet, which only added to his out-of-control reaction.

He couldn't count the number of times the guys involved with the arrest had teased him and chuckled over J.D.'s actions. They thought she had real Texas grit. Tonight, their opinion of her had gone up several notches.

He pulled into the driveway and cut the engine. If he were honest and looked at her actions from an unemotional viewpoint, he could see that in spite of her fears, she'd come up with a plan to disarm Allen.

But he couldn't look at it from an unemotional angle. Damn. He loved her. And wanted a life with her.

And, amazingly, she'd said she loved him, too. But he'd handled her declaration of love with all the finesse of a baboon. Her actions tonight, risking her life to save his, told him that J.D. held nothing back when she loved. Her career would never separate them.

The question was, had he already driven her off, or did he still have a chance?

The lights in the living room were on. That gave him hope. When he unlocked the door, J.D. jumped off the couch and whirled to face him.

"How did everything go?" she asked.

He breathed a sigh of relief. She was here. He still had a chance. "Fine. Austin police are picking up the rest of the gang as we speak."

He leaned back against the door. His heart was racing, his blood pumping so fast he was dizzy. He wanted to tell her he was sorry for acting like a jerk, that he loved her. He wanted to drag her down the hall and make hot, passionate love to her. Instead, he stood like a statue, frozen by fear.

"That's good." She didn't hold his gaze.

He scanned the room, settling on the cactus. Hadn't she destroyed that by shoving it in Allen's face? He pointed to it. "I thought..."

"I repotted it. I can't guarantee it will survive."

This was ridiculous. Why were they talking about some dumb plant when their lives were hanging in the balance? And yet, it seemed odd that she'd gone to the trouble of saving it.

His mouth was as dry as the cactus's desert home. "Why, J.D.?" He took one step forward. "Why did you repot it?"

She shrugged. "It was wrong to abandon it when I could so easily save it."

Was she telling him that what *they* had could be saved? He swallowed his fear and walked toward her. It was then he noticed the shopping bag sitting by the end of the sofa. He stopped beside it and glanced down. Her things were inside. His eyes locked with hers.

"The killer's been caught," she explained. "There's no reason for me to stay. I've called Emma. She said I could stay with her until I find a place of my own."

She said it in such a reasonable voice that he wanted to howl out his frustration.

He took a step toward her. "You're wrong, J.D."

Her chin came up. "I'm wrong about what?"

He grasped her shoulders. "There's no reason for you to leave."

"Luke—" She licked her lips in a nervous gesture, but that simple act nearly brought him to his knees. He pushed her down onto the couch.

Sitting beside her, Luke took her hands in his. "I'm sorry, J.D., for the way I handled things. It's just that I was so scared you might have been hurt—killed—I went berserk." With his fingers, he tipped up her chin. "I love you, Counselor, so much that I'm crazy with it, as I so aptly proved tonight. You're in my head and my heart. I don't want you to leave, J.D. Stay. Make this marriage real.''

Her eyes clouded with confusion. It gave him hope. If she wasn't sure about leaving, then he could convince her to stay. He tenderly held her face between his hands, and his eyes were warm and compelling. "I'm not like your dad, J.D.,'' he added, hoping that was the one thread of doubt that was holding her back.

Her fingers brushed over his cheek. "I know."

And she did. Tonight's incident made her confront an ugly truth. She'd judged all men by the standard set by her father and Allen. But Luke wasn't responsible for the sins of others. He'd proven time and again he was different. Trustworthy. A man who deserved to be loved and respected.

Her lips trembled. "I was scared, Luke. Scared Allen would kill us and I'd never have the chance to tell you I love you."

She went eagerly into his arms. His mouth covered hers, tasting, loving.

"I should've trusted you," she said between kisses. "If I'd thought about it, I would've known you had some sort of plan to capture Allen. My only excuse is that I didn't have a lot of time to think."

He eased her down onto the cushions. "Are you going to take me up on my offer to make this marriage real?" he asked, his lips traveling down her neck.

"It's been pretty real this last week," she said in a husky voice.

He looked down at her. "You know what I mean, Counselor. Let's make this a lifelong commitment."

The phone rang. Luke was tempted to ignore it.

"Answer it," J.D. commanded, sitting up. "It might be important." And she wasn't going anywhere.

He hopped to his feet and raced into the kitchen.

"No, Emma," J.D. heard Luke say. "She won't be coming tonight or any night."

His low chuckle told her that Emma had said something naughty. He leaned around the door. "Emma wants to know if you still want her to file those papers you talked about."

"Tell her to rip them up."

He hung up the phone and came back to the living room. "What was that all about?" he asked.

"That, Detective, was your last chance to escape this marriage."

Gathering her in his arms, he said, "Good. I'm hoping to stay hitched for the next fifty years."

Her expression grew serious. "I've got to warn you, Luke, that I don't intend to give up my practice. I still plan to work as a criminal defense attorney."

"Good, because I plan on being a cop the rest of my life. I'll supply you with plenty of clients."

"I don't doubt it."

The look in his eyes grew hot and steamy. "Then why don't we adjourn to the bedroom and seal this deal?"

Running her finger along his lower lip, J.D. said, "You know what, Luke? I believe you're a better wheeler-dealer than my dad."

"Count on it, Counselor."

* * * * *

HE'S AN

AMERICAN HERO

A cop, a fire fighter or even just a fearless drifter who gets the job done when ordinary men have given up. And you'll find one American Hero every month only in Intimate Moments—created by some of your favorite authors. This summer, Silhouette has lined up some of the hottest American heroes you'll ever find:

July: HELL ON WHEELS by Naomi Horton—Truck driver Shay McKittrick heads down a long, bumpy road when he discovers a scared stowaway in his rig....

August: DRAGONSLAYER by Emilie Richards—In a dangerous part of town, a man finds himself fighting a street gang—and his feelings for a beautiful woman....

September: ONE LAST CHANCE by Justine Davis—A tough-as-nails cop walks a fine line between devotion to duty and devotion to the only woman who could heal his broken heart....

AMERICAN HEROES: Men who give all they've got for their country, their work—the women they love.

IMHER05

INTIMATE MOMENTS®
Silhouette®

Take 4 bestselling love stories FREE

Plus get a FREE surprise gift!

Special Limited-time Offer

Mail to Silhouette Reader Service™

3010 Walden Avenue
P.O. Box 1867
Buffalo, N.Y. 14269-1867

YES! Please send me 4 free Silhouette Intimate Moments® novels and my free surprise gift. Then send me 6 brand-new novels every month, which I will receive months before they appear in bookstores. Bill me at the low price of $2.71 each plus 25¢ delivery and applicable sales tax, if any.* That's the complete price and—compared to the cover prices of $3.50 each—quite a bargain! I understand that accepting the books and gift places me under no obligation ever to buy any books. I can always return a shipment and cancel at any time. Even if I never buy another book from Silhouette, the 4 free books and the surprise gift are mine to keep forever.

245 BPA AJH9

Name	(PLEASE PRINT)	
Address	Apt. No.	
City	State	Zip

UMIOM-93R   ©1990 Harlequin Enterprises Limited

Premiere

Silhouette Books has done it again!

Opening night in October has never been as exciting! Come watch as
the curtain rises and romance flourishes when the stars of tomorrow
make their debuts today!

Revel in Jodi O'Donnell's STILL SWEET ON HIM—
Silhouette Romance #969
...as Callie Farrell's renovation of the family homestead leads her
straight into the arms of teenage crush Drew Barnett!

Tingle with Carol Devine's BEAUTY AND THE BEASTMASTER—
Silhouette Desire #816
...as legal eagle Amanda Tarkington is carried off by wrestler
Bram Masterson!

Thrill to Elyn Day's A BED OF ROSES—
Silhouette Special Edition #846
...as Dana Whitaker's body and soul are healed by sexy physical
therapist Michael Gordon!

Believe when Kylie Brant's McLAIN'S LAW —
Silhouette Intimate Moments #528
...takes you into detective Connor McLain's life as he falls for
psychic—and suspect—Michele Easton!

Catch the classics of tomorrow—*premiering* today—
only from **V**. *Silhouette*

**Relive the romance...
Harlequin and Silhouette
are proud to present**

by Request™

A program of collections of three complete novels by the most
requested authors with the most requested themes. Be sure to
look for one volume each month with three complete novels by
top name authors.

In June: **NINE MONTHS** Penny Jordan
                        Stella Cameron
                        Janice Kaiser

**Three women pregnant and alone. But a lot can
happen in nine months!**

In July: **DADDY'S   Kristin James
          HOME**   Naomi Horton
                       Mary Lynn Baxter

**Daddy's Home ... and his presence is long
overdue!**

In August: **FORGOTTEN   Barbara Kaye
             PAST**   Pamela Browning
                         Nancy Martin

**Do you dare to create a future if you've forgotten
the past?**

Available at your favorite retail outlet.

HARLEQUIN®   *Silhouette*

Fifty red-blooded, white-hot, true-blue hunks from every State in the Union!

Beginning in May, look for MEN MADE IN AMERICA! Written by some of our most popular authors, these stories feature fifty of the strongest, sexiest men, each from a different state in the union!

Two titles available every other month at your favorite retail outlet.

In September, look for:

DECEPTIONS by Annette Broadrick (California)
STORMWALKER by Dallas Schulze (Colorado)

In November, look for:

STRAIGHT FROM THE HEART by Barbara Delinsky (Connecticut)
AUTHOR'S CHOICE by Elizabeth August (Delaware)

You won't be able to resist MEN MADE IN AMERICA!
